**HARLEQUIN®**
*Presents*

Don't miss out on any of our books in March!

This month, Lynne Graham brings you
*The Italian Billionaire's Pregnant Bride,*
the last story in her brilliant trilogy THE RICH, THE
RUTHLESS AND THE REALLY HANDSOME, where
tycoon Sergio Torrente demands that pregnant Kathy
marry him. In *The Spaniard's Pregnancy Proposal*
by Kim Lawrence, Antonio Rochas is sexy,
smoldering and won't let relationship-shy Fleur
go easily! In Trish Morey's *The Sheikh's Convenient
Virgin,* a devastatingly handsome desert prince
is in need of a convenient wife who must be pure.
Anne Mather brings you a brooding Italian who
believes Juliet is a gold-digger in *Bedded for the
Italian's Pleasure.* In *Taken by Her Greek Boss*
by Cathy Williams, Nick Papaeliou can't understand
why he's attracted to frumpy Rose—but her
shapeless garments hide a very alluring woman.
Lindsay Armstrong's *From Waif to His Wife* tells the
story of a rich businessman who avoids marriage—
but one woman's sensual spell clouds his perfect
judgment! In *The Millionaire's Convenient Bride*
by Catherine George, a dashing millionaire needs
a temporary housekeeper—but soon the business
arrangement includes a wedding! Finally, in
*One-Night Love Child* by Anne McAllister, Flynn
doesn't know he's the father of Sara's son—but
when he discovers the truth he *will* possess her....
Happy reading from Harlequin Presents!

# QUEENS *of* R♥MANCE

*The world's favorite romance writers*

*New and original novels you'll treasure forever
from internationally bestselling
Presents authors, including:*

**Helen Bianchin**

*[signature]*

**Sandra Marton**

*[signature: Sandra Marton]*

**Emma Darcy**

*[signature: Emma Darcy]*

**Anne Mather**

*[signature: Anne Mather]*

**Lynne Graham**

*[signature: Lynne Graham]*

**Lucy Monroe**

*[signature: Lucy Monroe]*

**Penny Jordan**

*[signature: Penny Jordan]*

**Michelle Reid**

*[signature: Michelle Reid]*

**Miranda Lee**

*[signature: Miranda Lee]*

**Cathy Williams**

*[signature: Cathy M. Williams]*

# Anne Mather

## BEDDED FOR THE ITALIAN'S PLEASURE

## QUEENS *of* R♥MANCE

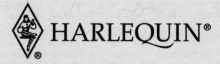

## HARLEQUIN®

TORONTO • NEW YORK • LONDON
AMSTERDAM • PARIS • SYDNEY • HAMBURG
STOCKHOLM • ATHENS • TOKYO • MILAN • MADRID
PRAGUE • WARSAW • BUDAPEST • AUCKLAND

ISBN-13: 978-0-373-12710-8
ISBN-10:     0-373-12710-3

BEDDED FOR THE ITALIAN'S PLEASURE

First North American Publication 2008.

www.eHarlequin.com

**Printed in U.S.A.**

All about the author...
*Anne Mather*

I've always wanted to write—which is not to say I've always wanted to be a professional writer. For years I wrote only for my own pleasure, and it wasn't until my husband suggested that I send one of my stories to a publisher that we put several publishers' names into a hat and pulled one out. The rest, as they say, is history. And now, more than 150 books later, I'm literally—excuse the pun—staggered by what's happened.

I wrote all through my childhood and into my teens, the stories changing from children's adventures to torrid gypsy passions. My mother used to gather these up from time to time, when my bedroom became too untidy, and dispose of them! The trouble was, I never used to finish any of the stories, and *Caroline,* my first published book, was the first book I'd actually completed. I was newly married then, and my daughter was just a baby, and it was quite a job juggling my household chores and scribbling away in exercise books every chance I got. Not very professional, as you can see, but that's the way it was.

I now have two grown-up children, a son and daughter, and two adorable grandchildren, Abigail and Ben. My e-mail address is mystic-am@msn.com and I'd be happy to hear from any of my readers.

# CHAPTER ONE

JULIET wondered what it was like in the Caymans at this time of year. Pretty much like Barbados, she assumed. They were all islands in the Caribbean, weren't they? But she'd never been to the Caymans.

Still, whatever they were like, they had to be better than this gloomy employment agency, whose sickly green walls and wafer-thin carpet were a poor substitute for the comfort she was used to. Had been born to, she amended, fighting back the tears of self-pity that formed in her eyes. Beautiful violet eyes, her father used to call them. They reminded him of her mother, who'd died when she was just a baby. How long ago it all seemed.

One thing she knew, her father would never have allowed her to be duped by a man like David Hammond. But her father, too, had died of a brain tumour when Juliet was just nineteen and a year later David had seemed like a knight in shining armour.

If only she'd realised that his main interest in her was the trust fund her father had left her. That just a handful of years after their society wedding he'd take off with the woman he'd introduced to Juliet as his secretary. With her stupid indulgence, he'd taken charge of her trust fund. By the time she'd realised what was happening, he'd transferred the bulk of it to an offshore account in his own name.

She'd been so naïve. She'd let David's good looks and boyish charm blind her to any faults in his character. She'd believed he loved her; ignored the advice of friends when they'd told her he'd been seen with someone else. Now the few pounds he'd left in their joint account were running out fast.

Of course, those friends that had stuck by her had been sympathetic. They'd even offered to help her out financially, but Juliet had known their friendship couldn't last under those circumstances. No, she had to get a job; though what kind of a job she could get with no qualifications she dreaded to think. If only she'd continued her education after her father died. But David's appearance in her life had blinded her to practical things.

She glanced round the waiting room again, wondering what sort of qualifications her fellow applicants had. There were five other people in the room besides herself: two men and three women, all of whom seemed totally indifferent to their surroundings. If she didn't know better, she'd have said they were indifferent to being offered employment, too. At least two of them looked half-asleep—or stoned.

Which could be good news or bad, depending on the way you looked at it. Surely after interviewing someone dressed in torn jeans or a grungy T-shirt, or that girl whose arms were covered with lurid tattoos, Juliet, in her navy pinstripe suit and two-inch heels, would be a relief. Or perhaps not. Perhaps unskilled jobs were more likely to be offered to people who didn't look as if they could afford to be out of work.

'Mrs Hammond?'

It's Ms Lawrence, actually, Juliet wanted to say, but all her means of identification were still in her married name. Not that everyone who got divorced reverted to their previous identity. But Juliet had wanted to. She'd wanted nothing to remind her that she had once been Mrs David Hammond.

Now she got nervously to her feet as the woman who'd called her name looked expectantly round the room. 'That's me,' she said, aware that she was now the centre of attention. She tucked her clutch bag beneath her arm and walked tentatively across the floor.

'Come into my office, Mrs Hammond.' The woman, a red-head, in her forties, Juliet guessed, looked her up and down and then led the way into an office that was only slightly less unprepossessing than the waiting room. She indicated an upright chair facing her desk. 'Sit down.' Juliet did so. 'Did you fill in the questionnaire?'

'Oh—yes.' Juliet produced the sheet of paper she'd been rolling into a tube as she waited. When she laid it on the woman's desk— Mrs Maria Watkins' desk, she saw from a notice propped in front of her—it remained in its half-curled position and she offered a little smile of apology as Mrs Watkins smoothed it out. 'Sorry.'

Her apology was neither acknowledged nor accepted. Mrs Watkins was too busy reading what Juliet had written, pausing every now and then to glance at her as if she couldn't believe her eyes. So what? Had the slick business suit fooled her? Or was she admiring Juliet's dress sense? Somehow, she didn't think so.

'It says here that you're twenty-four years old, Mrs Hammond.' Mrs Watkins frowned. 'And you've never had a job?'

Juliet coloured a little. 'No.'

'Why not?'

It was straight question, but Juliet had the feeling she shouldn't have asked it. She had some pride. Did this woman have to rob her of every single drop?

Taking a deep breath, she said, 'Is that relevant? I need a job now. Isn't that enough?'

'No, I'm afraid it's not, Mrs Hammond. Would-be employers require CVs; references. It's important for me to understand why a would-be applicant has none of these things.'

Juliet sighed. 'I was married,' she said, deciding that was the least controversial thing she could say.

'Yes, I see that.' Mrs Watkins consulted the sheet again. 'Your marriage ended some nine months ago, did it not?'

Nine months, eight days, recited Juliet silently. 'That's right.'

'But no job?'

'No. No job.'

Mrs Watkins sucked in a breath through her nostrils that was clearly audible. It was the kind of sound her father's butler, Carmichael, used to make when he disapproved of something she'd done. That Mrs Watkins disapproved of her lack of experience was obvious. Juliet wondered if she would have fared better if she'd come in a grungy shirt and jeans.

'Well,' Mrs Watkins said at last, 'I have to tell you, Mrs Hammond, it's not going to be easy finding you employment. You have no discernible qualifications, no employment history, nothing in fact to convince an employer that you're a good worker. And trustworthy.'

Juliet gasped. 'I'm trustworthy.'

'I'm sure you are, Mrs Hammond, but in this world we don't work on word-of-mouth. What you need is an erstwhile employer to vouch for you, someone who is willing to commit his opinion to paper.'

'But I don't have an erstwhile employer.'

Mrs Watkins gave a smug smile. 'I know.'

'So you're saying you can't help me?'

'I'm saying that at the present time, I don't have a vacancy you could fill. Unless you wanted to wash dishes at the Savoy, of course.' She chuckled at her own joke. Then she sobered. 'You'll find details of courses you could take at the local college—classes for everything from cookery to foreign languages—in the waiting room. I suggest you take a few of the leaflets home and decide what it is you want to do. Then, come back and see me when you feel you have something to offer. Until then, I'd advise you not to waste any more time.'

Waste *my* time, was what she meant, Juliet decided gloomily, getting to her feet. 'Well—thank you,' she said, the good manners, which had been instilled into her since birth by a series of nannies, coming to her rescue. 'I'll think about what you've said.' She paused. 'Or find another agency.'

'Good luck!' The latter was said with some irony and Juliet left the office feeling even more of a pariah than before. But what had she expected? Who had she imagined would employ someone without even the sense to recognise a con man when she saw one?

Outside again, she looked up and down Charing Cross Road, considering her options. Although it was only the beginning of March, it was surprisingly warm, though a light drizzle had started to dampen the pavements. She lifted a hand to hail a taxi and then hastily dropped it again. The days when she could swan around in cabs were most definitely over.

Sighing, she started to walk towards Cambridge Circus. She would catch a bus from there that would take her to Knightsbridge and the tiny one-bedroom apartment where she lived these days. The large house in Sussex where she'd been born and lived for most of her life had been sold just after her marriage to David. He'd said the house he'd found in Bloomsbury was much more convenient. It wasn't until he'd left her that she'd found out the house had been rented by the month.

She knew her friends had been appalled at her naïvety, but, dammit, she'd never encountered David's kind of ruthlessness before. It was just luck that the apartment had been in her name and David couldn't touch it. It had been her father's *pied-à-terre* when he'd had business to attend to in town, and she'd hung on to it for sentimental reasons.

Halfway to her destination she passed a pub and on impulse she went in. It was dark and smoky in the bar, but that suited her. She hardly ever drank during the day and she'd prefer it if no one recognised her in her present mood.

Slipping onto one of the tall stools, she waited for the bartender to notice her. Short and fat, with a beer belly that hung over his belt, he managed to look both businesslike and cheerful. Much different from Mrs Watkins.

'Now, then,' he said, sliding his cleaning cloth along the bar, 'what can I get you?'

Juliet hesitated. It didn't look as if it was the kind of place that had a bottle of house white waiting to be poured. But who knew?

'The lady would like a vodka and tonic, Harry,' said a voice at her shoulder and she swung round, ready to tell whoever it was that she could choose her own drinks, thank you very much.

Then her eyes widened in surprise. She knew the man. His name was Cary Daniels and she'd known him since they were children. But she hadn't seen him for years. Not since her wedding, in fact.

'Cary!' she exclaimed. 'Goodness, fancy seeing you here.' The last she'd heard he was living in Cape Town. 'Are you on holiday?'

'I wish.' Cary slid onto the empty stool beside her, handing a twenty-pound note to the bartender when he brought their drinks. He'd apparently ordered a double whisky for himself and he swallowed half of it before continuing. 'I've got a job in London now.'

'Really?'

Juliet was surprised. Although they'd lost touch for a few years, when his parents died and he'd had to go and live with his paternal grandmother in Cornwall, he had attended her wedding. At that time he'd been excited about the great job he'd got with the South African branch of an investment bank and everyone had thought he was set for life. But things had changed, as they do. Didn't she know it?

'So how have you been?' he asked, pocketing his change and turning on his seat to face her. Although the dim light had prevented her from noticing before, now she saw how haggard he looked. There were bags beneath his eyes, his hair was receding rapidly, and his thickening waistline told of too many double whiskies over the years. She knew he was twenty-eight, but he looked ten years older. What had happened to him? she wondered. Was he suffering the after-effects of a bad relationship, too?

'Oh—I'm OK,' Juliet said lightly, lifting her glass in a silent salute and taking a sip. It was much stronger than she was used to and she just managed to hide a grimace. 'Getting by, I suppose.'

'I heard about your divorce.' Cary was nothing if not direct. 'What a bastard!'

'Yes.' There was no point in denying it. 'I was a fool.'

'I wish I'd been around when it happened. He wouldn't have got off so lightly, I can tell you. What's the son of a bitch doing now?'

Juliet pressed her lips together. It was kind of Cary to be so supportive, but she couldn't see him tackling someone like David. He simply wasn't the type. 'Um, David's in the Caymans, or so I believe,' she admitted reluctantly. 'But do you mind if we don't discuss it? There's no point in harbouring old wounds. I was a fool, as I said. End of story.'

'You were gullible, that's all.' Cary was assertive. 'As we all are from time to time. It's easy to be wise after the event.'

Juliet gave a rueful smile. 'Isn't that the truth?'

'So—what are you doing?' Juliet tried not to resent his curiosity. 'And where are you living? I guess the house in Sussex has had to be sold.'

'Yes.' Juliet acknowledged this. 'I've got a small apartment in Knightsbridge. It used to be Daddy's and it's not the Ritz, but at least it's mine.'

'Bastard!' said Cary again. Then, 'I suppose you've had to get a job.'

'I'm trying to,' said Juliet honestly. 'But I've got no qualifications. I don't even have anyone I could apply to for a character reference. Except friends, of course, but I wouldn't do that to them.'

'Ah.' Cary swallowed the remainder of his drink and signalled the barman that he wanted another. He gestured towards Juliet's glass, too, but she shook her head. She'd barely touched the drink. 'So—do you have any plans?'

'Not yet.' Juliet was getting tired of talking about her problems. 'What about you? Are you still working for the bank?'

'No such luck!' Cary reached for his second whisky and

downed a generous mouthful before going on. 'I've been black-balled by the banking community. Hadn't you heard? I'm surprised you didn't read about it in the papers. It was all over the financial pages.'

Juliet was tempted to say that she'd had other things to do than study the financial pages, but she was disturbed by what he'd said. 'What happened?'

Cary grimaced. 'I gambled with clients' funds and lost a packet. The bank was down a few million dollars and I was lucky to escape without being charged with negligence.' He lifted a careless shoulder. 'Apparently Grandmama still has some pull in financial circles. I was just chucked out of the bank with a severe slap on the wrist.'

Juliet was amazed. 'But a few million dollars!' she echoed disbelievingly.

'Yeah. I don't do things by halves.' He took another mouthful of his drink. 'It sounds a hell of a lot more in South African rand, let me tell you. But, dammit, you're encouraged to take risks and I took 'em. I guess I'm not such a clever dealer, after all.'

Juliet shook her head. 'I don't know what to say.' She paused. 'Was your—was Lady Elinor very cross?'

'Cross!' Cary gave a short laugh. 'She was livid, Jules. Positively fire-breathing. She'd never approved of my chosen career, as you probably know, and getting thrown out of South Africa pretty well burnt my boats with her.'

Juliet looked down at the liquid in her glass. She remembered Lady Elinor Daniels very well. Mostly because when Juliet was thirteen she'd been quite a frightening figure. She remembered feeling sorry for Cary, too, whose parents had disappeared while sailing in the Southern Ocean. At seventeen, he'd been taken away from everything and everyone he was used to, forced to go and live in some old house in Cornwall with a woman he barely knew.

Juliet lifted her head. 'But you say you've got another job?'

'A temporary one, yeah.' Cary scowled. 'Believe it or not, I'm working in a casino. Oh, not handling money. They've got more sense than that. I'm what you'd call a meeter and greeter. A kind of—bouncer, with class.'

Juliet gasped. 'I can't believe your grandmother approves of that.'

'She doesn't know. As far as she's concerned I've got an office job. She still hasn't given up hope of me settling down with a good woman and taking over the running of the estate. And that low-life, Marchese, is just waiting for me to put a foot wrong.'

Juliet would have thought he'd already put more than one foot wrong, but she didn't say so. 'Marchese?'

'Rafe Marchese!' exclaimed Cary half-irritably. 'Surely you remember? My aunt Christina's deliberate mistake?'

'Oh, your cousin,' said Juliet, understanding. But Cary took offence at that.

'The bastard,' he corrected. 'A real one this time. Surely you don't expect me to be friendly towards him. He's made my relationship with Grandmama almost impossible over the years. I don't forget how he treated me when I first went to live at Tregellin.'

'He's older than you, isn't he?'

'A couple of years. He must be thirty now. Or maybe a little older. Whatever, he's there all the time, like a thorn in my side, and Grandmama loves to taunt me about leaving the estate to him.'

'To taunt you?'

'Yeah. Not that she would, of course. Leave the place to Marchese, I mean.' Cary laughed again. 'She's far too conventional for that.'

Juliet hesitated. 'If your aunt was never married to his father, why is his name Marchese?'

'Because she put his father's name on his birth certificate.' Cary was dismissive. 'A bit of a joke, that, considering I don't think Carlo even knew he was going to be a father. Christina was such a flake, always taking off for some new destination, finding one distraction after another.'

'I thought she was an artist,' said Juliet, trying to remember what her father had told her.

'She'd have liked to think so,' said Cary, with a sarcastic smile. 'Anyway, like me, Rafe was orphaned at a fairly early age. One too many Martinis for Christina and she fell from the balcony of the hotel in Interlaken where she was staying with her latest conquest.'

'How awful!' Juliet was amazed that he could be so blasé about it. She had been his aunt, after all. She took another sip of her drink, taking a surreptitious glance at her watch as she did so. It was time she was leaving. She needed to buy one or two items of food from the local delicatessen before heading home.

'Anyway, I've got to go down there next week,' Cary went on, apparently unaware that she was getting restless. He grimaced. 'I told her I'd got a girlfriend and she wants to meet her.'

'Oh.' Juliet smiled. 'Well, I hope she likes her. Is it someone you met while you were in Cape Town, or does she live in London?'

'I don't have a girlfriend,' declared Cary flatly. 'I just told her that to get her off my back. You know what I said about her wanting me to settle down and so on? I thought if she believed I was getting serious about someone, she'd lay off for a bit.'

'Oh, Cary!'

'I know, I know.' He scowled and summoned the bartender again to order another drink. 'Where am I going to find a suitable girlfriend between now and next Thursday? I don't even know any "suitable" girls. My tastes run in another direction entirely.'

Juliet stared at him. 'You're—gay?'

'Hell, no!' Cary snorted. 'But the kind of girls I like, you don't take home to introduce to your grandmama. I'm not interested in settling down, Jules. I'm only twenty-eight. I want to have some fun. I don't want some good woman and a couple of sprogs hanging about my feet.'

Juliet shook her head. He'd changed so much from the shy boy he'd been when they were children. Was this his grandmother's doing, or had he always had this streak of selfishness in him? Perhaps he wasn't so different from David, after all.

She was suddenly aware that he was staring at her now. There was a distinctly speculative look in his eyes, and she hoped he had no designs as far as she was concerned. She might be desperate, but Cary simply wasn't her type. Sliding down from her stool, she nodded pointedly towards the door.

'I've got to go.'

'Go where?'

Was it any of his business? 'Home, of course.'

Cary nodded. 'You wouldn't fancy having dinner with me, I suppose?'

'Oh, Cary—'

'It was just a thought.' He chewed vigorously at his lower lip. 'I wanted to put a proposition to you. But I can do it here, just as well.'

'Cary—'

'Hear me out.' He laid a hand on her sleeve and, although Juliet badly wanted to pull away, she had accepted a drink from him and that made her briefly in his debt. 'Would you consider coming down to Tregellin with me? As my *pretend* girlfriend,' he added swiftly, before she could object. 'You say you need a job. Well, I'm offering you one. Well-paid, of course.'

Juliet couldn't believe her ears. 'You're not serious!'

'Why not? We're friends, aren't we? We're male and female. Where would be the harm?'

'We'd be deceiving your grandmother. And—your cousin.'

'Don't worry about Rafe. He doesn't live at the house.'

'All the same—'

'You'd be doing me the greatest favour, Jules. And

Grandmama is bound to believe it when she sees it's you. You know she's always liked you.'

'She hardly knows me!'

'She knows *of* you,' persisted Cary. 'And when we get back, I'll be able to write you a reference you can use to get another job.'

'A real job, you mean?'

'This is a real job, Jules, I promise you. Oh, please. At least say you'll think it over. What have you got to lose?'

# CHAPTER TWO

THE tide was in and the mudflats below Tregellin were hidden beneath a surge of salt water. There were seabirds bobbing on the waves and the sun dancing on the water was dazzling. For once, the old house had an air of beauty and not neglect.

It needed an owner who would look after it, Rafe thought, guiding his mud-smeared Land Cruiser down the twisting lane that led to the house. Though not him, he reminded himself firmly. Whatever the old lady said, she was never going to leave Tregellin to the illegitimate son of an olive farmer.

Not that he wanted her to, he reflected without malice. Now that the studio was up and running, he hadn't enough time to do what he had to do as it was. Oh, he collected the rents and kept the books, made sure the old lady paid her taxes. He even mowed the lawns and kept the shrubbery free of weeds, but the house itself needed a major overhaul.

The trouble was, he didn't have the money. Not the kind of money needed to restore the place to its former glory anyway. And if Lady Elinor was as wealthy as the people in the village said she was, she was definitely hiding it from her family.

He knew Cary thought his grandmother was a rich woman. That was why he seldom refused an invitation, ran after her as if her every wish was his command. It was pathetic, really. If Rafe had had more respect for the man he'd have told him the old lady was just using him to satisfy her lust for power. If she did intend to make Cary her heir, she was going to make him work for it.

Whatever happened, Rafe doubted Tregellin would survive another death in the family. Unless Lady Elinor had some hidden cash that no one knew about, when she was gone the estate would have to be sold. It was probably Cary's intention anyway. Rafe couldn't see his cousin moving out of London, giving up the life he had there. Nevertheless, with death duties and lawyers' fees, Rafe suspected he'd be lucky to clear his grandmother's debts.

Rafe was fairly sure the old lady had been living on credit for some time. The tin mines, which had once made the Daniels' fortune, had been played out and dormant for the past fifty years. The estate, with its dairy farms and smallholdings, had struggled in recent years. Things were improving but, like everything else, they needed time.

Time they might not have, he acknowledged. It was sad, but the old lady wasn't as robust as she'd once been. He hated to think of what might happen when she died. Tregellin deserved to be resurrected. Not sold to fund another loser's debts.

He skirted the tennis court and drove round to the front of the house. Tregellin faced the water. It occupied a prime position overlooking the estuary. When he was a kid he used to love going down to the boathouse, taking out the old coracle Sir Henry had taught him to use.

He pushed open his door and got out, hauling the bag of groceries he'd bought at the local supermarket after him. Lady Elinor wouldn't approve of him spending money on her, but Josie would. Josie Morgan was the old lady's housekeeper-cum-companion, and was almost as old as Lady Elinor herself.

Although he'd parked the Land Cruiser at the front of the house, Rafe followed the path that led round to the kitchen door. Hitchins, the old lady's Pekinese, was barking his head off as usual, but when Rafe came through the door he stopped and pushed his snub nose against Rafe's leg.

'Noisy old beast, aren't you?' Rafe chided him, bending to scratch the dog's ears with an affectionate hand. Hitchins was almost fourteen and blind in one eye, but he still recognised a friend when he saw one. He huffed a bit, wanting to be picked up, but Rafe dropped his bag on the scrubbed-pine table and started to unpack it instead.

Josie bustled through from the hall, carrying a tray, and Rafe saw an empty cafetière and two cups, and a plate that still contained three chocolate digestives. He picked up one of the biscuits and bit into it as Josie welcomed him, making light of her thanks as she examined what he'd brought.

'Fillet steak!' she exclaimed with some enthusiasm. 'You spoil us, Rafe, you really do.'

'If I don't, who will?' he retorted philosophically. 'How is the old girl this morning? I intended to get over yesterday evening, but then I got caught up with something else.'

'The something else wouldn't be called Olivia, would she?' she teased him, putting the steak and other perishables he'd brought into the ancient fridge.

'You've been listening to too much gossip,' retorted Rafe, stowing a warm loaf in the bread bin. 'Where is the old lady, anyway? I'd better go and say hello.'

'Shall I bring another pot of coffee?' Josie paused in what she was doing, but Rafe just shook his head.

'I'll take one of these,' he said, picking up a can of ginger ale he'd bought for his own use when he was here. 'No. No glass,' he deterred her, when she would have taken one from the cupboard. He paused. 'The conservatory, right?'

'Oh—yes.' Josie pulled a rueful face and tucked a strand of iron-grey hair behind her ear. 'She'll have heard the car, I don't doubt for a minute. She may be old but her hearing's as sharp as ever.'

Rafe grinned, and with Hitchins at his heels he walked across the mahogany-panelled hall and into the morning room opposite. Beyond the morning room, a vaulted conservatory basked in sunlight. It was built at one side of the old house, to take advantage of a view of the river. Weeping willows trailed their branches in water that mirrored their reflection, while kingfishers dived from the river bank, their speed only equalled by their success.

Lady Elinor was seated in a fan-backed basketwork chair beside a matching table. The morning newspaper resided on the table, turned to the crossword that was almost completed. It was the old lady's boast that she could finish the crossword before eleven o'clock every morning and, glancing at his watch, Rafe saw she still had fifteen minutes to go.

'Don't let me keep you!' she exclaimed shrewishly, noting his momentary distraction, and Rafe pulled a face before bending to kiss her gnarled cheek.

'I won't,' he assured her. 'I was just checking the time, that's all. It looks like it's in danger of defeating you today.'

'If you're talking about the crossword, that fool, Josie, has kept me gossiping again. She brings my coffee and then thinks she has to keep me entertained. I've said to her a dozen times, I don't need her company.'

'You love it really.' Rafe was laconic. He picked up the Pekinese and walked across to the French windows, gazing out across the river to the meadows beyond. 'So—what have you been talking about? Or am I not supposed to ask?'

'Since when has that stopped you?' Lady Elinor was impatient. 'I was telling her that Cary's bringing his fiancée to meet me on Thursday. I'm hoping they'll stay for a few days. At least over the weekend.'

'His fiancée, eh?' Rafe turned, and put the dog down again. Ignoring its complaints, he pushed his hands into the pockets of his leather jacket, a heavy strand of night dark hair falling over his eyes. 'That must please you. Him settling down at last.'

'If it's true.' The old lady massaged the handle of the malacca cane that stood beside her chair and Rafe thought how difficult it would be for Cary to put one over on his grandmother. Her brain was as sharp as it had ever been, despite the many wrinkles that lined her patrician features. 'I've met the girl, actually. She and her family lived in the same road as Charles and Isabel, when they were alive. Her name is Juliet Lawrence—well, it used to be Lawrence, but she's a divorcee, so who knows what she calls herself now? She's younger than Cary. Her father used to work in the City. Her mother died when she was just a baby and I believe her father died five or six years ago.'

'A comprehensive history,' remarked Rafe drily, and Lady Elinor gave him a darkling look.

'I need to know these things, Raphael,' she said irritably. 'I don't want Cary marrying some strumpet. At least this girl is from a decent family.'

Rafe shrugged. 'You don't think entertaining Cary and his girlfriend might be too much for you right now?' he ventured, and saw the look of indignation that crossed the old lady's face.

'I've had a cold, Raphael. Not pneumonia. It's the time of year. I always catch a cold in the spring.'

'If you say so.' Rafe knew better than to argue. 'OK. If that's all, I'll go and see if Josie needs any help. If you're putting them in the Lavender Room, I'd better check the bathroom for leaks.'

Lady Elinor looked positively offended. 'I'm not putting *them* anywhere,' she declared, laying great emphasis on the pronoun. 'Cary will stay in his own room, as usual, and Miss Lawrence can use Christina's apartments.'

Rafe's jaw tightened. 'I've never heard you call them that before.'

'Haven't you?' The old lady was dismissive. 'Christina was my daughter, Raphael. Just because she chose to live the kind of life I could never approve of doesn't mean that I've forgotten her.'

'Or forgiven her?'

'I'm too old to bear grudges, Raphael.'

'OK.' He inclined his head and strolled towards the door. 'Is there anything else you need?'

Lady Elinor pursed her lips. 'Josie told me that you had a reception at the studio last night,' she ventured, with some reluctance. 'Why wasn't I informed?'

Rafe sighed, pausing in the doorway, one shoulder propped against the frame. 'I didn't think you'd be interested.'

The old lady scowled. 'And why would you think that?'

'Why would I think that? Let me count the ways,' he misquoted mockingly. 'Because you don't approve of my painting portraits for a living? Because you don't want me to turn out like my mother? Because my independence sticks in your craw? Am I getting close?'

'I don't approve of some of the people you mix with,' conceded Lady Elinor testily. 'But I never stopped your mother from doing what she wanted, and I shan't attempt to stop you. Remember, it was she who chose to live in all those exotic places, hauling a small boy around whose existence I knew nothing of. When she died, however, I didn't hesitate in offering you a home here with me.'

Rafe's shoulders rounded. 'I know.'

'Just because we don't always see eye to eye—'

'Look, I'm sorry, OK?'

'—doesn't mean I don't care about you, Raphael.'

'I know.' Rafe closed his eyes for a moment and then said wearily, 'I should have told you about the reception. You're right, I was thoughtless. The local paper took some pictures, so when I get copies I'll show them to you. It wasn't a very grand affair. Just a glass of wine and a chance to view the studio.'

'I'm sure it was very exciting,' said Lady Elinor, but Rafe could hear the reluctance in her voice. 'Before long, you won't be spending any time at Tregellin at all.'

'I'll always have time for you, old lady,' retorted Rafe harshly. 'Look, I've really got to get moving. I'm meeting Liv Holderness at half-past twelve.'

'Olivia Holderness?' Lady Elinor's eyes narrowed. 'Would that be Lord Holderness' daughter?'

'Lord Holderness doesn't have a daughter,' said Rafe flatly. 'Or a son either, as you very well know. Liv's his wife. She wants to discuss having her portrait painted as a gift to her husband on his sixtieth birthday.'

'I see.' The old lady frowned. 'You seem very familiar with her. I seem to remember Holderness hasn't been married to her for very long.'

'Eighteen months, I think.' Rafe's tone was sardonic. He knew nothing went on in the surrounding area that Lady Elinor didn't hear about sooner or later. 'She's his third wife. The old guy turns them in at regular intervals for a new model.'

'Don't be coarse.' Lady Elinor was disapproving. 'And you be careful what you're doing, Raphael. It seems significant to me that she'd choose a local studio over any number of more famous establishments she and her husband must know in London.' .

Rafe grimaced. 'Damned with faint praise,' he said drily. 'Don't worry, I've known Liv for a few years. Her father owns the Dragon Hotel in Polgellin Bay.'

'Ah.' The old lady nodded. 'So she's one of the Melroses?'

'The youngest daughter,' agreed Rafe, wishing the old lady didn't make them sound like the Doones.

'So she's a lot younger than Holderness?'

Rafe nodded. 'About thirty years, I think. But they seem happy enough.'

'Well, you keep what I've said in mind,' declared Lady Elinor, unexpectedly getting to her feet and coming towards him. She was tall, though not as tall as he was, and leaning heavily on her cane. She was wearing her signature pleated skirt and silk blouse, with a heather-coloured shawl draped about her shoulders, and her once dark hair was now liberally threaded with grey. She laid a hand on his sleeve and looked up at him with eyes as blue as the gentians that grew higher up the valley. 'You take care,' she added, reaching up to kiss him. 'I may not always show it, but I'm very fond of you, Raphael.'

It was the electric bill that had done it.

It had been waiting for her when she'd got back to the apart-

ment and she'd stared at the figure she owed with wide disbelieving eyes. She couldn't believe she'd used that much electricity. For heaven's sake, she'd rarely used the oven and she'd
religiously turned out lights as she'd gone from room to room.

But she had used the microwave, she'd acknowledged. And
the underfloor heating system was expensive. A neighbour had
warned her of that. But seeing what she'd owed in black and
white had really scared her. The fact that it had been the heaviest
season of the year had been no consolation at all.

That was why, when Cary had rung two days later, asking her
if she'd reconsidered, she'd given in to his persuasion. The figure
he'd offered her for four days work had been impossible to
refuse. She'd known it would pay her immediate bills and leave
her a little bit over. Possibly enough to survive until she got a
proper job.

All the same, as Cary turned off the A30 just beyond Bodmin
on Thursday afternoon, Juliet couldn't deny the butterflies in her
stomach that were telling her she'd made a terrible mistake. She
liked Cary; of course she did. Or perhaps she'd used to like the
boy she'd known all those years ago. These days, she knew very
little about him. His attendance at her wedding hardly consti-
tuted grounds for a friendship.

And, despite the fact that he kept telling her she was going
to love the area where his grandmother's house was situated, the
idea of being introduced to Lady Elinor Daniels as Cary's
fiancée left an unpleasant taste in her mouth. When he'd first
broached the idea, he'd said he needed a girlfriend. Now it had
metamorphosed into a fiancée, which was a whole different ball
game.

'Not long now,' Cary said, taking her silence for tiredness.
'We could still stop for lunch, if you like. That would give us a
break.'

Juliet, who didn't want to spend any more time alone with
him than was necessary, managed a faint smile. 'We don't want
to be too late arriving,' she said, keeping her eyes on the road

ahead. 'Besides, didn't you say your grandmother is expecting us for lunch?'

Cary's mouth compressed and Juliet got the feeling that he wasn't looking forward to this visit any more than she was. Which was understandable, she supposed, if the old lady kept interfering in his private life. But, let's face it, she thought, without Lady Elinor's intervention he could be languishing in a South African prison. She'd read enough stories about rogue dealers who'd almost bankrupted the banks they'd worked for.

'I suppose it is a bit late now,' he conceded at last, and she realised he was responding to her question. Then, pointing away to the west, 'Have you ever seen sea that colour before? In England, I mean. It's almost tropical. It reminds me of a holiday I had in Mauritius. God, that was some hotel we stayed in. A whole floor given over to our suite.'

'Expensive,' murmured Juliet drily, and Cary turned to glance at her.

'Yeah, I wish I had that kind of cash now,' he agreed, without a trace of remorse. 'That's why I have to be so careful how I treat the old girl. Without her money, I'd be taking a package holiday in Spain every year.'

Juliet's eyes widened. 'Does she know you spend the money she gives you on expensive holidays?'

Cary frowned. 'Hey, that information's not for public consumption,' he said. 'Don't you be discussing my financial arrangements with her. If she chooses to sub me sometimes, I'm not going to refuse it, am I? The old girl's loaded! You might not think it to look at the house, but, believe me, I know she's got a fortune hidden away somewhere.'

Juliet was feeling less and less enthusiastic about her part in this deception. She told herself that if Cary had been totally honest with her from the beginning, she'd never have agreed to come. Or was she being totally honest with herself? she wondered. Damn it all, she was doing it for the money, too.

'Tell me about your cousin,' she said, trying to distract herself. 'What's he like? Does he look like you?'

Cary scowled. 'As if.' And then, when she was obviously waiting for him to go on, he muttered irritably, 'He looks like a gipsy, if you must know. Swarthy skin, greasy black hair and an attitude you could cut with a knife.'

Juliet's brows ascended. 'You really don't like him, do you?'

Cary shrugged. 'I've told you what he's like. Always ingratiating himself with the old woman. I've no doubt she'll sing his praises while you're here. She does it just to wind me up.'

'Oh, Cary—'

'I mean it. I've got better things to do than mend light switches and plug leaks. I'm a banker, Jules, not a labourer. Or rather I was until the futures market stuffed up.'

Juliet chose her words with care. 'He probably only does these things to help your grandmother. I mean, it isn't always easy to find a plumber or an electrician when you need one.'

'Yeah, well, he needn't think that doing all these things gives him some claim on the estate when the old lady snuffs it. As soon as the will's read, I'm going to tell him I don't want him trespassing on the place in future. Tregellin's mine. I'm the only legitimate heir and he knows it. But that doesn't stop him from hanging around, pretending he's helping her out.'

Juliet shook her head. 'You're so bitter!'

'No.' Cary wouldn't have that. 'Just practical. Anyway, we're almost there. That's the chimneys of the house you can see over the treetops. It's set on a promontory overlooking the Eden estuary. The River Eden, I mean.' He grimaced. 'It may be a beautiful spot, but it's no Garden of Eden.'

They approached the house down a winding track between hedges of rhododendron and acacia. Juliet guessed that in late spring and early summer these same hedges would be a riot of colour. Right now, the glossy leaves hid the buds of any blossoms, and because there were lowering clouds overhead it was rather gloomy.

The grounds of the house seemed quite extensive. A tennis court and a croquet lawn, a vegetable garden behind a lichen-covered stone wall. They circled the building and Juliet saw that it was the back of the house that faced the road. The front looked out across the river estuary, the water shallow now as the tide receded.

There was a big SUV already parked on the forecourt and as Juliet thrust open her door and got out she heard Cary give a grunt of irritation. Turning to see what had caused his annoyance, she saw that a man had just appeared from around the side of the house. He was a big man, tall and powerfully built, wearing a worn leather jacket and jeans that clung to lean muscular thighs. Scuffed boots completed his attire and Juliet didn't need a sixth sense to know that this must be the infamous Rafe Marchese.

He looked across the width of the courtyard towards her and she felt a disturbing flutter of awareness in the pit of her stomach. But goodness, he was attractive, she thought, realising that Cary's scornful description hadn't done the man justice.

His hair was dark, yes, and needed cutting, but it wasn't greasy. His skin was darkly tanned and there was the stubble of a beard on his jawline, but she wouldn't have called him swarthy either. He wasn't handsome. His features were too hard, too masculine for that. And she'd bet her last penny that it wasn't only for his technical skills that Lady Elinor liked having him around.

'Cary,' he said evenly, as the other man got out of the car, and Cary was obliged to acknowledge him in return.

'Rafe.' His voice was tight and he turned at once to take their luggage from the back of the car, making no attempt to introduce Juliet.

Which really annoyed her. More than it should, probably, she admitted, but dammit, she was supposed to be his fiancée. Deciding she didn't care what Cary thought, she walked around the bonnet of the car and held out her hand.

'Hi,' she said with a smile. 'I'm Juliet. Cary's—girlfriend.'

# CHAPTER THREE

THE lunch had been cold, but Juliet knew they couldn't blame the housekeeper for that. They'd been expected at one; they'd actually arrived at a quarter-past two. However expert the cook, no one could have kept a mushroom risotto hot indefinitely.

Not that she'd been particularly hungry. The encounter between Cary and Rafe Marchese had robbed her of her appetite somewhat. The two men obviously disliked one another, but Cary had behaved like a boor and she'd been sucked into his game.

Perhaps some of the blame was hers. She'd initiated his anger when she'd introduced herself to his cousin. But, dammit, she'd been angry with Cary for ignoring her and she hadn't thought about the possible consequences of her actions when she'd approached the other man.

The truth, however unpalatable, was that she'd wanted Rafe Marchese to notice her. Which was weird, considering that since David had walked out on their marriage over a year ago she'd had no interest in other men.

Not that she flattered herself that Marchese had felt the same way. He'd been polite, but distant, his first words succinctly delineating her reason for being there. 'Ah, yes,' he'd said. 'Cary's fiancée.' He'd paused. 'Lady Elinor was beginning to think you'd changed your minds.'

All the same, when he'd touched her hand she'd reacted as if she'd accidentally touched a hot wire. The heat that passed from his hand into hers shocked her to the core. Then she'd looked up into eyes that were as dark and brooding as the storm clouds massing over Tregellin and known that, whatever happened, she was already out of her depth.

Of course, she'd snatched her hand away, rather rudely, and Cary had come charging over, like some mad bull defending his mate. 'What's going on?' he'd demanded, laying a possessive hand on Juliet's shoulder. 'What have you been saying to my fiancée? As you apparently knew we were coming, I thought you'd have had the decency to stay away.'

Rafe Marchese didn't seem at all perturbed by Cary's bluster. 'It's good to see you, too, Cary,' he'd said, as faultlessly polite as before.

'Well…' Cary had been indignant. 'Grandmama told me how you're too busy for her these days. Spending time with your artsy-craftsy friends, was how she put it. But I might have known you'd be around when I was here.'

Rafe's lips had tilted humorously. 'I shouldn't take what the old lady says too seriously,' he'd remarked, his eyes lingering on Juliet's now burning face. 'You know she likes to play us off against each other. If you weren't such an easy mark, she'd never get away with it.'

'Oh, and you know her so well,' Cary had sneered, but Rafe had only lifted his shoulders in a self-deprecatory shrug.

'I'd say I see more of her,' he'd declared mildly. 'Whether that constitutes knowing her better remains to be seen.'

'Well, don't think I don't know what you're trying to do,' Cary had continued. 'You think that, because I live in London and you live here, you've got the advantage.' His hand had squeezed Juliet's shoulder. 'Once we're married, I think you can kiss any chance of changing her mind goodbye.'

Dear God, Juliet had wanted to die, she thought now as she unpacked her suitcase. For heaven's sake, it was bad enough pretending to be Cary's fiancée without him talking about them getting married as if it were going to happen in the next few weeks. She had no idea what Rafe Marchese had thought. If his mocking smile was anything to go by, he was used to Cary's bombastic behaviour and he didn't take offence from it. But she wished she hadn't been a part of it all the same.

The altercation had been thankfully brought to an end by the advent of a small dog. It was a little yapping Pekinese that had made straight for Cary and dug its teeth into his trouser leg. 'Damn stupid mutt!' Cary had exclaimed, kicking out angrily, sending the dog scuttling across the yard.

'He's actually quite intelligent,' Rafe had remarked coolly, bending to rescue the little animal, massaging its ears with a long-fingered brown hand that was lightly covered with dark hair. Juliet had felt a momentary envy for the dog, which was ridiculous. But then Cary had hauled their bags out of the car and headed for the house and she'd been obliged to follow him.

She guessed now that he hadn't wanted to argue with the animal. It was Lady Elinor's dog and Juliet doubted she'd appreciate learning that her grandson had kicked the Pekinese. It was to be hoped Rafe Marchese wouldn't tell her. Though after the way Cary had behaved, she wouldn't blame him if he did.

Meeting Lady Elinor again had been a bit of an anticlimax after the confrontation outside. She was a lot older than Juliet remembered, naturally, but she was still an intimidating figure. If anything, Juliet would have said that Rafe resembled her far more than Cary. He had her height and that same air of cool breeding.

During lunch, Juliet had had to fend off quite a number of questions about her failed marriage to David. The fact that it was only nine months since her divorce was finalised had elicited the opinion that in her position Lady Elinor wouldn't have been in any hurry to rush into marriage again.

Of course, Cary had come to her rescue, assuring the old lady that the reason Juliet's marriage hadn't worked was that she'd married the wrong man in the first place. 'Hammond was only after her money,' he'd said contemptuously, and Juliet had been glad Rafe Marchese hadn't been there to see the faintly amused expression that had crossed Lady Elinor's face at his words.

But at least it had given her a breathing space and, when the meal was over, she'd been relieved to hear her hostess bid Josie show their guest to her room. Evidently the old lady had wanted to spend some time alone with her grandson and Juliet prayed he wouldn't make any more promises he couldn't keep.

With her unpacking completed, Juliet contemplated the apartment she'd been given. It was much bigger than the rooms she was used to. Even the rooms at her father's house couldn't have competed with this. But the whole place was incredibly shabby; the high ceilings badly needed attention and the thick paper that must have once decorated the walls was now scuffed and peeling from neglect.

It was no wonder, really, if Josie was the only help Lady Elinor had. She was almost as old as her mistress, and Juliet doubted she had time to dust all the rooms, let alone attend to any repairs. Everything here was on a grand scale, including the furniture, and the bathroom next door sported a claw-footed tub and a lavatory that was elevated on a small dais.

Still, from the brief bounce she'd permitted herself on the bed, the mattress was comfortable. And the sheets were clean and smelled sweetly of a lavender-scented rinse. It was only for three nights, she assured herself. And Lady Elinor was unlikely to have anything more to say to her. Perhaps she could borrow Cary's car and drive into the nearest town. She had little money to do any shopping, but at least it would keep her out of the way.

The room was at the front of the house and she had a magnificent view over the river estuary. At present the tide was out and there were dozens of birds strutting over the mudflats, looking for food. She saw gulls and waders; she even recognised a pair of sandpipers. She was no expert, but she guessed you could get really interested in stuff like this if you lived here.

It was still only about half-past four and, deciding she couldn't stay in her room until suppertime, Juliet thought she'd go in search of the housekeeper. Perhaps Josie would tell her a little more about the history of the house—or the history of its occupants, she conceded, aware that she was more interested in Rafe Marchese than she was in anything or anyone else.

She rinsed her face at the crackled marble basin in the adjoining bathroom and then regarded her reflection in the spotted mirror. She still looked flushed, but that was probably just the cold water she'd washed with. Clearly Lady Elinor didn't believe in heating the water during the day.

In her bedroom again, after assuring herself that the cream silk jersey top and matching linen skirt she'd worn to travel in would do for her explorations, she reapplied eyeliner and mascara, brushing a bronze gloss over her generous mouth. She wasn't beautiful, she thought, but her heart-shaped features did have a certain appeal. Thankfully her hair, which was naturally curly, didn't require much more than a brush running through it. It bobbed just below the level of her shoulders and, although it was some time since she'd been able to afford highlights, there were still golden streaks in its honey-brown mass. Or were they grey? she fretted, leaning closer to the mirror. After what she'd been through, she wouldn't have been surprised.

She made her way to the head of the stairs and started down, keeping a wary eye open for either Cary or her hostess. She would prefer not to run into either of them just yet and, as the gloomy hall appeared to be deserted, she headed swiftly towards what she hoped was the kitchen. And found Rafe Marchese lounging on a corner of the pine table, sharing a pot of tea with the housekeeper.

Juliet didn't know who was the most surprised, herself or Josie. 'Why—Miss Lawrence,' she said awkwardly, getting up from her place at the table to face her. 'I was just about to bring up your tea.'

'My tea?'

Juliet now saw the tray that had been prepared and left on one of the cabinets. There was a cup and saucer, milk and sugar, and a plate containing wafer-thin cucumber sandwiches and tiny butterfly cakes. Only the teapot was missing and she guessed Josie had been interrupted by her visitor.

If Rafe was disconcerted by her sudden appearance, he didn't show it. He didn't even get up, she noticed, merely raised the mug he was drinking from to his mouth and regarded her enigmatically across the rim.

'Yes, your tea.' Josie was anxious to assure her guest that it was all ready for her. 'But as you're down, would you like me to serve it in the drawing room instead?'

'Oh—um—' after the fiasco of lunch, Juliet had no desire to repeat the experience '—couldn't I just have it here? With you and—Mr Marchese.'

'Rafe,' he said flatly, putting his mug down on the table. He had no desire to get to know this young woman any better than he did already, but he couldn't ignore her. 'I think Josie would prefer it if you allowed her to serve you in the drawing room.'

Juliet's lips pursed. 'And I'd prefer to have it here,' she insisted smoothly. 'Is there a problem with that?'

'Of course not, Miss Lawrence.' Josie was clearly disturbed by the sudden hostility between them. 'If you'll just give me a minute to boil the kettle and make some fresh tea—'

'What you're having is fine.' Juliet sent Rafe a challenging look. Then, with what he thought was a reflection of his cousin's arrogance, 'I thought you'd left, Mr Marchese.'

'I came back,' said Rafe calmly. Then, mimicking her defiance, 'Do you have a problem with that?'

Her cheeks darkened with becoming colour, proving she wasn't as confident as she'd like to appear. 'It's not my place to comment,' she retorted tartly, but he couldn't let her get away with that.

'But you have,' he pointed out, picking up his mug again, and Josie clasped her hands together in dismay.

'Rafe, please,' she said, her eyes wide and appealing. 'I'm sure Miss Lawrence was only making conversation.' She hurriedly took the cup and saucer from the tray and lifted the teapot she'd been using. 'How do you like your tea, Miss Lawrence? With milk and sugar or a slice of lemon?'

Juliet felt embarrassed. There'd been no tension in the room when she'd arrived, but there was now. And it was all her fault.

Well, maybe not entirely her fault, she defended herself, as Josie added to her cup the milk that she'd requested. She was beginning to wonder if Cary might have some justification for his resentment after all. There was no doubt that Rafe was being deliberately awkward with her.

'Is your room comfortable?' Josie asked, offering Juliet a seat—and a way out—and, although she would have preferred to remain standing, she realised the old woman wouldn't sit down again unless she did.

'Um—very comfortable,' she said, casting another glance at Rafe as she pulled out a chair and sat down. 'It has a marvellous view of the estuary.'

Rafe watched her through narrowed eyes, wishing the old lady hadn't put her in his mother's old room. Wondering, too, what a girl like her would see in a loser like Cary. What had Lady Elinor told him? That she'd already been married and divorced? She didn't look old enough to have had so much experience of life.

Juliet was aware of him watching her, lids lowered, lashes to die for shading those disturbing dark eyes. What was he thinking? she wondered. Did he assume that like Cary she was only interested in the old lady's money? For, despite what he'd said to his cousin, she'd seen the expression on Cary's face when he'd thought Lady Elinor wasn't looking, and it hadn't been pleasant.

The silence had gone on too long and Josie, who had evidently been trying again to think of something non-contentious to say, turned appealing eyes to Rafe. 'Your grandmother's having a small dinner party on Saturday night. Did she tell you?'

Rafe's mouth compressed. 'Now why would she tell me a thing like that?' he queried drily. 'I'm not invited, am I?'

'N—o.' Josie had to be honest. 'But the Holdernesses are coming.'

'Are they?' He pulled a wry face. 'The old girl must be pulling out all the stops.'

'Well, that's the thing…'

But Josie belatedly seemed to realise she'd gone too far in a guest's presence and, meeting her troubled eyes, Rafe took his cue and said, 'Well, don't worry. I'll be around if you need me.'

'Oh, Rafe!'

The words were said with such heartfelt emotion that Juliet realised that, whatever she thought of him, the housekeeper didn't share her view. In fact, there seemed to be a genuine affection between them and Juliet permitted herself another look in his direction.

Only to encounter his reflective gaze.

She looked away immediately, but not before she'd gained the impression that his opinion of her was no less critical than hers of him. He evidently did think she was some empty-headed bimbo who'd only latched on to Cary because of his expectations.

As if!

Deciding it was up to her to try and change that impression, she forced herself to meet his gaze again and say politely, 'Cary said something about you being an artist, Mr Marchese. Should I have heard of you?'

'I believe what he actually said was that I had artsy-craftsy friends,' murmured Rafe rather maliciously, and heard Josie's sudden intake of breath.

'Rafe!' she exclaimed again, barely audibly, but Juliet wasn't listening to her.

'And do you?' she countered. 'Have artsy-craftsy friends, I mean?'

Rafe sighed, putting down his empty mug and regarding her tolerantly for once. 'No,' he said flatly. 'That's just Cary's way of denigrating anything he doesn't understand.'

'Please, Rafe…'

Josie was getting desperate and this time Juliet did hear her. 'Oh, don't worry, Mrs Morgan,' she said, giving the housekeeper a quick smile of reassurance. 'Mr Marchese doesn't like me. That's obvious. Well, that's OK. I'm not especially fond of him either.' She finished her tea and set down her cup. 'If you'll excuse me, I think I'll take a look outside, if that's permitted?'

When she emerged into the hall again, Cary was just coming down the stairs. Oh, great! she thought. That was all she needed. And the situation wasn't improved when the door behind her opened again. For some reason, Rafe had chosen to follow her.

Someone—Cary, she assumed—had turned on some lights and the hall didn't look half as gloomy as it had done when she'd come downstairs. In fact, with what appeared to be a Waterford crystal chandelier picking out the reddish grain in the panelling, a little of its former grandeur had been restored.

The angle of the stairs meant that Cary didn't immediately notice his cousin. 'Where've you been, Juliet?' he demanded peevishly. 'I've been looking for you for ages. I went to your room, but you weren't there. Obviously.' He waved an impatient hand. 'What the hell have you been doing?'

If Juliet had hoped that Cary's words might deter Rafe from interfering, she was mistaken. 'She's been having tea in the kitchen, with me and Josie,' he drawled lazily, stepping into the light. 'I assume you have no objections?'

'Like hell!' Cary had reached the bottom of the stairs and now he looked suspiciously from Juliet to the other man. Then, scowling at his supposed fiancée, 'How did that come about?'

Juliet sighed. 'By accident,' she said tersely, flashing Rafe an exasperated look. 'I was looking for—for someone to talk to. I thought Josie might be able to tell me a bit more about the house.'

'So what was he doing?' Cary cocked his head towards Rafe.

'I was having tea with Josie, if it's any business of yours,' replied Rafe before Juliet could answer. 'This isn't your house yet, Cary. I come and go as I please.'

'Don't I know it?' Cary sounded aggrieved. 'So where's the old girl? In the conservatory, as usual.'

'I imagine she's resting.' Rafe spoke with evident reluctance. 'She usually rests in the afternoon, as you'd know if you spent more time at Tregellin.'

Cary didn't bother answering him. Instead, he placed an arm about Juliet's shoulders, causing a rather unpleasant shiver to ripple up her spine. He bent his head towards her. 'How about you and me taking a walk in the grounds?' he suggested. 'I'd like to show you around.'

'Oh—no.' With some discretion, Juliet managed to ease herself out of Cary's reach. 'I—er—I was just thinking of taking a bath.'

She heard Rafe's disbelieving exhalation of breath and determinedly avoided his gaze. It wasn't anything to do with him if she chose to change her mind.

'A bath, eh?' Was Cary being deliberately provocative? she wondered. 'Oh, yeah, that sounds like a plan. We could take a bath together, baby. Have you noticed how big the tubs are here? It makes you wonder what the people of Great-Grandmama's generation used to get up to when Great-Great-Grandpapa used to throw those wild house parties between the wars.'

'Not what you're imagining, Cary,' declared a cool, aristocratic voice from the direction of the morning room. Lady Elinor was standing in the open doorway, the little dog, Hitchins, tucked under her arm. 'Rafe.' She nodded towards her other grandson. 'A minute before you leave, if you please.'

# CHAPTER FOUR

JULIET had a bath, but it was a fairly cold one. The only shower was hand-held, and she used it to sluice herself down before stepping out onto the marble floor. Fortunately, she'd laid a towel beside the bath before getting into it. She was already shivering, and imagining bare feet on cold marble didn't bear thinking about.

There was no hair-drier, but she'd washed her hair that morning, so that didn't worry her. Nevertheless, she wished she'd brought her own drier with her. She'd been spoiled, she thought. She was used to staying in hotels where every amenity was provided.

Not any longer, of course, she told herself, the spectre of the electricity bill briefly rearing its ugly head. And, however awkward it was for her here, at least it would provide her with enough money to pay it. If she could just ignore Rafe Marchese, it wouldn't be all that bad.

With the knowledge that Lady Elinor was giving a dinner party for her grandson on Saturday evening, Juliet studied the clothes she'd brought with her rather critically. It wasn't that she was short of clothes. On the contrary, until David had cancelled her credit cards, shopping had been something she enjoyed. But she hadn't brought a lot of clothes with her. Cary's complaint that his grandmother never spent any money hadn't prepared her for the real situation at Tregellin. Although the old lady might not have a lot of money, she lived in some style. The upkeep of the house alone had to be excessive, but there seemed to be no question of her leaving it and moving to smaller premises.

Which meant Juliet had to save her little black dress until Saturday. It was the most formal thing she'd brought, and when she'd tucked it into her case back in London she'd had real doubts about bringing it. She was glad she had now. Cary would expect his 'fiancée' to wear something suitable.

That evening she decided to wear a pair of cropped trousers in aubergine silk, whose low waist exposed a generous wedge of creamy skin. She'd wear a mauve and green patterned top with the trousers, its smock style successfully covering the breach.

It was a little after seven when she went downstairs. Cary had told her before they'd parted in the hall that his grandmother usually had supper at half-past. Although she would have preferred to stay in her room until it was time to eat, that would have been impolite, and, hearing the sound of voices from the drawing room, she headed in that direction.

The housekeeper was on her way out as Juliet entered the room, and after wishing their guest a good evening she hastened on her way. Expecting to find Cary with his grandmother, Juliet was perturbed to find it was just the two of them, though the old lady was graciousness itself as she offered her guest a sherry before the meal.

'Oh…' Juliet had never liked sherry, finding it too sweet, usually, but good manners dictated that she accept Lady Elinor's offer. 'Thank you.'

'Perhaps you'd help yourself,' added the old lady, gesturing with her cane towards the tray on the nearby bureau. 'I have a little arthritis in my hands and I don't find it easy lifting the decanter.'

Juliet nodded and went to do as she'd been asked, grateful that she need only pour herself a small amount. 'My father suffered from arthritis in his hands, too,' she said, coming to sit on the leather sofa opposite the old lady's armchair. 'He used to say it was with holding a pen for so many years.'

Lady Elinor acknowledged this. She was looking particularly elegant this evening in an ankle-length black skirt and a cream silk blouse. Once again, a shawl was draped about her shoulders, a Paisley pattern this time in autumn shades.

'Your mother died before your father, didn't she?' she remarked, and Juliet conceded that this was so.

'She died just after I was born. My father was devastated, as you can imagine.'

'Of course.' Her hostess absorbed this. 'And your father was considerably older than your mother, I believe,' she went on, startling Juliet by her knowledge. 'But at least he had you. You must have been very close.'

'Yes, we were.' Juliet felt a twinge of the distress she'd suffered when her father had died. Then, frowning, 'Did you know my father, Lady Elinor?'

'No.' The old lady shook her head. 'But I remember my son and his wife talking about Cary's friendship with Maxwell Lawrence's daughter. And I know Cary was dismayed when I removed him from all the friends he'd had in the village.'

Juliet took a tentative sip of her sherry and found it wasn't as sweet as she'd anticipated. 'That seems such a long time ago.'

'Well, of course, it is.' Lady Elinor sighed. 'It's easier to look back when you're my age.' She paused. 'But you married someone else. Cary attended your wedding. Did you realise you'd married the wrong man?'

Juliet pulled a wry face. 'You could say that.'

'You'd prefer not to talk about it?'

'No.' Juliet bit her lip. 'It was just a stupid mistake, that's all. David never loved me. As Cary probably told you, he was only interested in my money.'

Lady Elinor's brows drew together. 'And your father didn't insist that he sign some kind of agreement before you became his wife?'

'My father died a year before I met David,' explained Juliet ruefully. 'And as I say, I believed him when he said that money didn't matter to him.'

'Money always matters,' declared the old lady firmly. 'Except perhaps to someone like Rafe.' She paused. 'You've met Rafe, haven't you? He's my daughter Christina's son. Unfortunately she was never married to his father.'

'Ah.' Juliet pressed her lips together for a moment. 'May I ask what you meant when you said Rafe wasn't interested in money?'

It was a personal question, but happily the old lady didn't appear to take offence. 'Perhaps I should amend that to *my* money,' she said, with a wry smile. 'He does extremely well without it. The small gallery he's just opened in Polgellin Bay has proved quite a success.'

Juliet's eyes widened. 'So he is a painter?'

'He paints,' agreed Lady Elinor consideringly. 'He also teaches art at a comprehensive school in Bodmin.'

'Really?' Juliet realised Rafe had been deliberately vague on the subject. 'How interesting!'

'You think so?' The old lady sounded as if she had her doubts. 'His mother broke my heart with her—reckless disregard for propriety. She painted, too, and look what happened to her.'

'Cary said she—fell from the balcony of an hotel.'

'Well, that's the official story, anyway.'

Juliet stared at her. 'It's not true?'

Lady Elinor smiled a little drily. 'Ah, that would be telling, wouldn't it, Miss Lawrence? Why don't you tell me how you and Cary came to meet again? It seems such a coincidence. Do you visit the casino, by any chance?'

'The casino?' Juliet was taken aback.

'Yes. That is where my grandson works, isn't it?' She pulled a wry face. 'I can't imagine how he persuaded them to employ him after the fiasco he was involved in in South Africa. You know about that, I suppose?'

'Well, yes.'

Juliet didn't know what else to say and for once she was relieved to hear heavy footsteps crossing the hall. A moment later Cary appeared in the doorway, somewhat overdressed in satin-seamed black trousers and a dark red dinner jacket.

He came into the room with a slight swagger, as if he expected to be complimented on his appearance. But all Lady Elinor did was raise her dark eyebrows at him. And when Hitchins, who had been asleep in his basket at her feet, awoke and started growling, she bent and lifted the little animal onto her lap.

'Grandmama.' Cary greeted her politely, gave the dog a less-friendly look and then came to seat himself beside Juliet. 'You're looking delectable this evening,' he said, bestowing an unwelcome kiss on her neck just below her ear. 'Hmm, and you smell delectable, too. Is it Chanel?'

'No.' Juliet refrained from saying that it was a simple herbal essence that wasn't half as expensive. 'Your grandmother and I have been waiting for you.'

'Sorry.' Cary would have kissed her again, but Juliet managed to avoid it. 'If I'd known you were missing me, I'd have been much quicker, believe me.'

'She didn't say she'd been missing you, Cary,' observed the old lady a little maliciously. 'As a matter of fact, Juliet and I have been having a very interesting conversation.'

'You have?' Cary looked a little uneasy now.

'Yes.' His grandmother smiled her satisfaction. 'She was just about to tell me where the two of you renewed your acquaintance.'

Juliet sighed, aware that Cary had stiffened beside her. This was an eventuality they hadn't covered, though she realised in hindsight it had been foolish not to do so. 'We—er—we met at the home of mutual friends,' she lied, the glance she cast in Cary's direction warning him not to contradict her. 'It was the Bainbridges, Cary, wasn't it? John and Deborah. We've both known them for years.'

'Yes, the Bainbridges,' agreed Cary gratefully, but Juliet,

hearing the falseness in his tone, could well understand why
Lady Elinor had chosen to investigate his employment for
herself. It was to be hoped the old lady wasn't a friend of the
Bainbridges, too. Debbie would be most confused to hear that
Juliet was planning on getting married again without telling her.
Not to mention meeting her future fiancé at her house.

'And that was when?'

The old lady wasn't finished yet and this time Cary intervened. 'Oh—it must be over six months ago!' he exclaimed ex-
pansively, inspiring a silent groan from Juliet.

'Over six months?' queried his grandmother at once, as
Juliet had known she would. 'So why haven't I heard anything
about it? When you were down—let me see, six weeks ago—
you made no mention of the fact that you were thinking of getting engaged, Cary.'

Cary looked blank-faced now and Juliet knew that, once
again, she'd have to come to his rescue. 'That was my fault, Lady
Elinor,' she lied, hoping her smile would hide her blushes. 'I'm
afraid I asked Cary to keep our relationship to himself. With it
being such a comparatively short time since my divorce, I didn't
want anyone to think I was rushing into marriage again.'

The older woman's lips thinned. 'Even though you are,' she
commented drily, and Juliet gave a rueful shrug. But, fortunately, Josie returned at that moment to say that supper was
ready and Cary got gratefully to his feet.

The rest of the evening progressed without further embarrassment. Juliet couldn't decide whether Lady Elinor had been satis-
fied with the answers they'd given her or merely biding her time
until morning. Whatever, the meal—roast beef and Yorkshire
pudding with a fruit compote for dessert—passed without incident,
and afterwards Juliet had the perfect excuse to retire early.

'It's been a very long day,' she said, when Cary chose to
question her departure, and, meeting her narrowed gaze, he evidently decided not to push his luck.

'Yeah, you get a good night's rest,' he said, catching her hand as she passed him and raising it to his lips. 'I'll see you in the morning, darling. Sleep well.'

In fact, Juliet slept only fitfully. Although the bed was comfortable, it was a strange bed, and the knowledge that there were still three more days to go weighed heavily on her mind. After tossing and turning for hours she eventually rose just as the sky was lightening, padding barefoot across to the windows and peering out.

The view was calming. Sunrise on the estuary, and the mudflats were a veritable hive of activity. She'd never seen so many birds in one place before, cackling and squawking as they vied with one another for the grubs the receding tide had left behind.

It looked as if it was going to be a fine day. The clouds, such as they were, were thinning, and a delicate haze was lifting to reveal a pale blue horizon. Juliet knew a sudden urge to be outside, far from another round of interrogation. For no matter how amiable Lady Elinor had been the night before, she was fairly sure her curiosity hadn't been totally assuaged.

In the bathroom, the hand shower ran lukewarm, but it was better than nothing. Chilled, but refreshed, Juliet dressed in jeans and a V-necked olive-green sweater, pulled on Converse boots, and left her room.

As on the night before, there seemed to be no one about, which wasn't really surprising. It was barely seven o'clock. Much too early for Lady Elinor to want breakfast.

The kitchen was chilly. The Aga, which had evidently kept the place warm the afternoon before, was cold now and blinds still covered the windows. Juliet opened the blinds and, locating the kettle, set it to boil. If she could just find a jar of instant coffee, she thought, she'd be happy.

She found what she was looking for in the third cupboard she opened, and by then the kettle was boiling. She put two teaspoons of coffee in a mug and then filled it with hot water. Then she turned to a rather elderly fridge, looking for milk.

She had her back to the door when a key turned in the lock and it opened. She swung round in surprise to find Rafe Marchese letting himself into the house. He was carrying a couple of bags and the delicious aroma of newly baked bread came to her nostrils. She had thought she wasn't hungry, but she'd been wrong.

'Making yourself at home?' he remarked lazily, putting the bags down on the pine table. He was wearing khaki cargo pants this morning and a navy body-warmer over an open-collared Oxford shirt. There was a disturbing glimpse of dark body hair showing in the opening, and his shirtsleeves were rolled back to display forearms that were deeply tanned and also spiced with hair.

Juliet felt herself going red as she looked at him. Honestly, she thought with annoyance, you'd think she was a foolish virgin who'd never dealt with men before. Which was so untrue. What was it about Rafe Marchese that made her think about things any decent girl would be appalled by?

'Um—do you want some?' she asked, trying to sound cool and collected, when she was anything but, and Rafe's lips curved in amusement.

'It depends what you're offering,' he said, watching as the hot colour flamed in her cheeks.

She was certainly easy to watch, he thought. Easy to disconcert, too, which was interesting. This morning she was wearing jeans that hugged the sexy contours of her hips, and, although she persistently pulled her sweater down, it kept inching up to display a tantalising glimpse of creamy skin.

She was certainly nothing like the woman he'd expected when the old lady had told him that Cary was bringing his fiancée to Tregellin. And, although common sense told him it would be unwise to bait her, there was something about her that aroused a malicious desire to see how far he could go.

For her part, Juliet knew he was being deliberately provocative, and she wondered why. Dammit, she was a divorced woman, and supposedly Cary's fiancée besides. Did he know she was hopelessly out of practice when it came to men like him?

'Coffee,' she replied now, with heavy emphasis, and, as if taking pity on her, he grinned.

'If you mean that—stuff—you're drinking, I'll pass, thanks,' he said, pulling various bakery products out of the bags. 'Josie makes filter coffee. The equipment's around here somewhere.'

'I hope you don't expect me to make you special coffee!' exclaimed Juliet indignantly, and he arched a mocking brow in her direction. 'What are you doing here, anyway?' she persisted, refusing to let him daunt her. 'Isn't it a bit early to be making a social call?'

Rafe sucked in a breath. 'This is your idea of being sociable?' He propped his lean hips against the drainer, crossed his feet at the ankles and folded his arms. Then, regarding her with dark, assessing eyes, he added, 'Remind me to avoid you when you're feeling touchy. Or is that tetchy?' He grimaced. 'One or the other.'

Juliet pursed her lips. 'You didn't answer my question.'

'What question was that?'

Juliet knew he knew damn well what question, but she played along. 'I asked what you were doing here so early in the morning. Did Lady Elinor send for you?'

Rafe looked down at the toes of his boots before answering her. Then he said, 'In a manner of speaking,' not wanting to explain exactly why he was here.

'Why?'

'Why what?'

'Why did she send for you?' If he could be provocative, so could she. Then a thought occurred to her. 'She's not ill, is she?'

Rafe's lids lifted and he looked at her again with those dark, disturbing eyes that caused such an insistently hollow ache in the pit of her stomach. 'Not that I know of, anyway,' he remarked. Then, casually, 'Did you have a pleasant evening?'

Juliet blew out a breath. She felt as if she'd been running fast and not getting anywhere. He was being purposely obtuse and she didn't know how to penetrate his mocking façade.

'It was—very pleasant,' she said at last, resisting the urge to expand upon her words. She took a sip of her coffee. 'Hmm, this is good.'

'Yeah, right.'

Rafe didn't believe her, but he really didn't have the time to prove it to her right now. Rubbing a hand over the incipient beard on his jawline, he straightened away from the unit and said, 'D'you want a croissant? They were made fresh this morning and I can vouch for that.'

Juliet was tempted, but she wasn't sure it would be wise to take anything from him. Her tongue circled her lips. 'Did you make them?'

Rafe gave a short laugh. 'No,' he said, for once being straight with her. 'I didn't get to bed till one a.m., so I certainly wasn't up at five o'clock making pastry.'

One o'clock! Juliet would have loved to ask what he'd been doing until that time, but she didn't have the courage to go that far. Besides, he'd probably been with some woman, and did she really want to know?

Instead, she said, 'OK,' unable to deny the lure of the delicious-smelling roll. It was so long since she'd been able to afford such a treat.

The pastry crumbled in her fingers and tiny flakes flecked her lips as she struggled to get it into her mouth. She looked incredibly sexy and Rafe knew an unexpected desire to lick the pastry from her lips with his tongue. She wasn't wearing any make-up this morning, and he sensed her mouth would be soft and wet and sweet-smelling—

*Dios!* He arrested his thoughts at that point. She was Cary's girlfriend, for pity's sake. What was he thinking of, allowing himself to get a hard-on when there was absolutely no chance of him easing it with her? If he had any sense, he'd keep her at arm's length.

Juliet had put down her cup to take the pastry and now she

pulled a paper towel from the roll and wiped her lips. 'That was—fantastic!' she said, and meant it. 'Thank you.'

'My pleasure,' Rafe returned, aware that she was looking at him with much less hostility now. Evidently his generosity had had the opposite effect on her and it would be fatally easy to change his mind.

But, to his relief, he heard the sounds of activity from upstairs. Josie's rooms were above the kitchen and dining room, and Rafe guessed she'd either heard his car or their voices. Probably the latter.

Keeping his tone deliberately light now, he said. 'So—what are you and Cary planning on doing today?'

Juliet picked up her cup, took a sip, and set it down again. 'I don't know.' She pulled a wry face. 'Believe it or not, before you arrived I was intending to go for a walk. Maybe along by the river.'

Rafe regarded her assessingly. 'In those boots?'

Juliet glanced down at her feet. 'They're very comfortable.'

'But not exactly waterproof,' observed Rafe drily. 'You need rubber boots. The river bank is very muddy at this time of year.'

'Oh, well…' Juliet shrugged her slim shoulders, causing her hair to bounce against her neck. 'I suppose I'll just have to confine my explorations to the garden.' She paused. 'Are you—teaching today?'

Rafe's brows drew together. 'The old lady told you that, I suppose?'

'That you teach? Yes.' Juliet frowned. 'It's not a secret, is it?'

'No.' But she could tell he didn't like the idea that they'd been talking about him. 'You'll find that Lady Elinor prefers the thought of me pursuing regular employment to making my living in some other way.'

'Painting, you mean?'

He grinned without malice and her stomach twisted in response. He was so damn attractive and she wouldn't have been human if she hadn't been aware that being single again had definite disadvantages. It was so long since she'd either had, or wanted to have, sex with a man, least of all David. But the idea of Rafe's hands on her body caused goose bumps to feather her skin.

Not that it was likely to happen, she reminded herself. Apart from the fact that he wasn't interested in her, she was supposed to be Cary's girlfriend. There was no way he was going to forget that, however much she might wish he would.

'Yeah, painting,' he said now, just as Josie came into the kitchen. Her sharp eyes took in their presence and the bakery bags lying open on the table. And Rafe found himself feeling guilty. As if the thoughts he'd been having were somehow visible on his face.

'You're up early, Miss Lawrence,' she said, addressing herself to Juliet first, and Juliet gave a rueful smile.

'It was such a lovely morning,' she said, even though she'd had no idea what it was like when she'd first got out of bed. 'I thought I might go for a walk.'

'And I delayed her,' put in Rafe pleasantly. 'She needs rubber boots and she doesn't have any.'

'What size shoes do you take, Miss Lawrence?' asked the housekeeper, bending to open what appeared to be a flue. Juliet realised then that the Aga hadn't been dead, as she'd imagined. As soon as Josie opened the vents, it roared to life again.

But they were waiting for her answer, and forcing herself to concentrate, she said, 'Um—five-and-a-half, I think.'

'Then you can borrow my boots, if you want to,' declared Josie triumphantly. She straightened, resting a hand on the curve of her spine as though it pained her. 'They're a six, but if you add a couple of pairs of socks, they should do.'

Juliet didn't know what to say. She'd never had to borrow anyone's boots before, but this was not the time to be choosy. 'That's awfully kind of you,' she said. 'And, please, call me Juliet. Yes, I'd like to borrow your boots, if you don't mind?'

# CHAPTER FIVE

RAFE arrived home soon after noon. His apartment was over the small studio where he exhibited his own, and occasionally other artists' work. It had been a dream of his when he was growing up to open his own premises. And, although the rewards were small, he got a great deal of satisfaction out of it.

He'd had a class at the school where he worked part-time that morning. But this afternoon, Liv Holderness was coming to the studio so he could make some provisional sketches for her portrait. He sometimes used a camera to get a perspective on his subject. He needed to assess height and depth and the kind of lighting that would be needed. Photography was another subject he'd become fairly expert in, though painting was his first love.

In his apartment, which comprised a large living and dining area, a small kitchen, bedroom and bath, he flung off his body-warmer and went to make himself some coffee. Spooning the grounds into the filter, he was reminded of his early-morning encounter with Juliet Lawrence. Irritation stirred in his gut. Dammit, what was it about that woman that bugged him so? She'd been reasonably polite, friendly almost, but he'd behaved like a jerk.

To begin with, anyway, he amended, remembering how he'd provoked her. And, really, he'd prefer not to think about the way he'd reacted later. Letting her get under his skin had been pathetic. Apart from anything else, she was Cary's fiancée. And from what he'd learned from Lady Elinor, it didn't sound as if she'd done a decent day's work in her life.

According to the old lady, she'd been the pampered only child of a wealthy businessman. She'd gone straight from finishing-school into marriage, apparently becoming a pampered wife. The reasons the marriage hadn't worked out weren't so easy to fathom. Irreconcilable differences, he assumed, switching on the coffee-maker. Wasn't that the current jargon when couples got bored with one another and wanted to move on?

Why she would attach herself to Cary Daniels was another mystery. Unless she was one of those females who needed a masculine hand to hold. After all, she was—what?—twenty-something, with no evident desire for independence. Didn't she care that Cary went through money like a knife through butter?

Whatever, it was nothing to do with him, he reminded himself. Thank God, he had his own life and could make a comfortable living without anyone's help. That was one of the things that annoyed the old lady. Lady Elinor would have much preferred him to be like his cousin. As it was, she could rarely catch him on the raw.

He'd brought a ciabatta sandwich home with him. Shades of his father, he thought wryly. He'd always liked Italian bread. It was filled with smoked ham and cheese and he was enjoying it with his second mug of coffee when Olivia arrived. Shoving its remains into his small fridge, he put down his mug and went to answer the door.

Olivia Holderness was nothing like Juliet Lawrence. Though, once again, why he should be making a comparison annoyed the hell out of him. Just because Liv was a busty blonde, who liked to wear short skirts and high heels to draw attention to her shapely legs, was no reason to criticise her. Yet that was what he was doing, he recognised. Comparing her with a woman who might be tall and slim and classy, but didn't have half Liv's charm.

Nevertheless, he wasn't in the best of moods when he

escorted Liv downstairs again and into his studio. The place was closed to the public when he was working. Unlike some painters, Rafe didn't like an audience. Besides, any serious collectors tended to make an appointment, and Rafe's main source of income was commissioned stuff.

'I can only stay an hour,' Olivia was saying conversationally as he seated her in the chair he intended to use to get perspective. 'Bobby thinks I'm at the hairdresser's,' she added as Rafe adjusted the lights he was angling to expose her face. She giggled. 'I'm going to have to make some excuse when he notices my hair still looks the same as it did. What do you think?'

Rafe was still getting his head round the fact that 'Bobby' was Lord Robert Holderness. It was easy to forget that Liv was Lady Holderness now, despite the way she looked. She'd confided that Bobby had fallen in love with her because she was so different from his other wives. And that Rafe could readily believe.

'My hair looks all right, doesn't it?' She was persistent. 'I mean, I want it to look good in the portrait.' She giggled again. 'Imagine me having my portrait painted! I mean, who'd have thought it?'

Rafe found himself smiling. 'Who indeed?' he remarked drily, and she gave him a flirtatious look.

'You don't think I'm silly?'

'No. Why would I? You're paying me very well and I need the work.'

'Now, I happen to know that's not true.' Olivia pressed her lips together thoughtfully for a moment. 'Poppy—that's Poppy Gibson,' she added, mentioning the name of the wife of the local member of parliament, 'she told me she'd been at your reception last week and you'd been offered quite a few commissions. I just wish Bobby and I had been able to come. But he wasn't feeling so good—he has blood pressure, you know—and I couldn't leave him on his own, could I?'

'Definitely not.'

'And you think my hair looks all right?' She touched the straightened strands that dipped provocatively to the exposed curve of her breast. 'Connie—that's Conrad Samuels at Batik in Bodmin—thinks I suit this colour. But I'm not sure. I'm a natural blonde, you know?'

'Yeah, right.' Rafe was sarcastic. He'd known her long enough to be aware that her hair was naturally brown. Like Juliet's, he thought, though without the shine he'd noticed just that morning. He scowled. God, he had to get that woman out of his head.

'There's no need to look like that.' Olivia had taken his scowl for a response to what she'd been saying. 'Anyway, Bobby thinks I'm a natural blonde and that's what matters.'

'Does he?' Rafe's mouth quirked up at the corners. 'Now, that surprises me.'

'You devil!' Olivia jumped up from the chair and punched his arm. 'I bet you can't remember what I look like. It was dark that night and you were—well—'

'Drunk,' supplied Rafe drily, pushing her back onto the seat. 'Now, sit still, will you? We're wasting your time and mine.'

'But it was good, wasn't it?' Olivia was determined to continue their conversation. 'I remember waking up the next morning and thinking I was in love.'

'In lust more like,' countered Rafe, not wanting to have this conversation. His association with Liv had been short and not especially sweet. He remembered waking up with a hangover. Much like the one he'd got this morning, he thought, but with a legitimate cause.

'But we were good together,' she persisted. And when he didn't answer, she shook her head in annoyance. 'Rafe, are you listening to me?'

He'd just lined up his camera when she shifted and ruined the shot. 'I'm listening,' he said through his teeth. 'But I'm trying to work here. If you'd wanted to chat, you should have asked me out for a drink.'

Olivia's jaw jutted. 'I'm sorry if I'm being a nuisance,' she said huffily, and Rafe only just managed to suppress his groan.

'You're not a nuisance,' he assured her. 'Take no notice of me. I had too many glasses of wine last night.'

'Wine?' Olivia arched neatly plucked brows. 'Since when do you drink wine, Rafe?'

'Since I discovered it's a cheaper analgesic than Scotch,' he informed her flatly. Then, after studying her through the lens of his camera for a moment. 'Are you sure about this? You really think your husband will approve?'

'Me being painted in the nude?' Olivia looked smug. 'Oh, yes. Bobby's nuts about my body.'

'OK.' Rafe knew better than to argue, but he hoped she was right. 'So—you want the whole shebang? Belly button, boobs and butt?'

Olivia grimaced at him. 'You have such a charming way of putting it.' She folded her hands in her lap, tugging at the hem of her skirt, pretending that she didn't want him to notice her legs. And they were very attractive legs, Rafe had to admit. He hoped he could do them justice.

'Fine.'

He adjusted the camera again, taking several shots from different angles. This was useful to learn the structure of her face, the shape of her head, the curve of her neck. He was aware of her watching him, following his movements with her eyes, a look of anticipation on her face. And wondered, not for the first time, if accepting this commission had been entirely wise.

'OK,' he said after a few minutes, stowing the camera on a side-table and tugging a velvet couch into the middle of the floor. 'Come and make yourself comfortable on this. I want to make a few sketches, just to get an idea of how it's going to look.'

Olivia got immediately to her feet. 'Shall I take all my clothes off?' she asked eagerly, her fingers going to the buttons of her skirt.

'*No!*' Rafe's response was emphatic and Olivia gave him a resentful look. 'That is,' he hastened on in an effort to redeem himself, 'it's not necessary today. These are just preliminary sketches. I'll fill in the details later. It's amazing how much can be done without the subject's participation.'

Olivia pouted. 'Won't I have to take my clothes off at all?'

'Not initially, no.' Rafe sighed. 'You should be grateful. This is a draughty old place at the best of times.'

'I suppose.' But Olivia still looked disappointed and Rafe realised she'd wanted to strip for him. Oh, God, he thought, surely the old lady wasn't going to be proved right. When Lady Elinor had poured scorn on the credentials of the new Lady Holderness, perhaps he should have listened...

Juliet spent a pleasant couple of hours trudging along the river bank. Upstream, she'd discovered that it wasn't a particularly wide river. Indeed, in places the trees growing on the opposite bank hung so far across the water that they almost touched those on this side. The ground, as Rafe had warned her, was thick with mulch, the accumulation of last autumn's windfall and months of heavy rain.

The air near the estuary was salty, but further upstream it was overlaid with the smell of rotting vegetation. Yet, spring was definitely stirring. She wished she knew more about the wild flowers that grew in such profusion along the stream.

When she got back to the house, she discovered that Cary and his grandmother were having morning coffee in the conservatory. Juliet, who'd changed out of Josie's boots in the mudroom, would have preferred to hurry upstairs and tidy herself before meeting her hostess again. But Cary had evidently been looking out for her and he came to the door of the morning room as she was hastening across the hall.

'Where've you been?' he asked at once, just as he'd done the evening before. 'If you'd planned on going out, you might have told me.'

'I didn't exactly plan it,' said Juliet, not wanting to get into how she had come to go out in the first place. She ran a hand over her tumbled hair. 'I just went for a walk, that's all. And, as you can tell, the wind was fairly strong.'

'Even so, you should have told me,' Cary insisted in a hushed voice. 'I'd have appreciated the chance to get a breath of fresh air after the atmosphere in this mausoleum.'

'I'm sorry.'

'Well, never mind. You're here now. Come on in. We're having coffee in the conservatory.'

'Oh, well—I was just going to tidy up,' she protested, but Cary didn't seem to care about her feelings. Or her appearance, for that matter.

'Later,' he said, taking hold of her elbow and guiding her into the morning room. 'Here, take off your coat. We don't want the old girl thinking you were about to make a break for it.'

'As if!'

Juliet gave him an impatient look, but Cary was intent on his objective. 'Here she is, Grandmama!' he exclaimed triumphantly, leading her into the conservatory. 'I thought she was still in bed, but apparently she's been for a walk.'

Before Juliet could speak, however, Hitchins came hurtling across the floor. He'd apparently been sleeping in his basket, as usual, but Cary's loud voice had disturbed him. As before, he made straight for Cary's trouser leg, and she could see his frustration at not being able to do anything about it.

'Hey…' With a smile of greeting for Lady Elinor, Juliet bent and detached the Pekinese from his quarry. Evidently he had no quarrel with her, because when she lifted him into her arms he immediately licked her chin. 'Now, you won't get around me that way,' she said, even though she was touched by the little dog's affection. 'That was naughty. We don't go around biting people, do we? It's not polite.'

The old lady had been watching this exchange with some interest. 'He likes you, Miss Lawrence,' she said. 'He's usually a good judge of character, I find.'

Which Cary evidently didn't find easy to deal with. The smug smile he'd been wearing while Juliet was holding the dog now gave way to a petulant scowl. But he didn't say anything, she noticed. He just shoved his hands in his trouser pockets and pretended he hadn't understood what the old lady was saying.

Deciding it was up to her to answer, Juliet scratched the dog beneath his chin. 'I used to have a golden retriever,' she said. 'When I was much younger. And, please—my name is Juliet. I'd be happy if you'd use it.'

'Juliet.' Lady Elinor nodded and pointed to the wickerwork armchair adjacent to her own with her cane. 'Come and sit down, Juliet. And I think you can put Hitchins down, too. If Cary will just stop waffling about, the dog will simply ignore him.'

'I'm not waffling about, Grandmama.' Cary's tone was defensive, if anything. He paused. 'Shall I go and ask Josie for another cup for Juliet? Then you and she can have a nice chat.'

Juliet, who'd just sat down, raised horrified eyes to his face. But there was nothing she could say that wouldn't sound rude, and he knew it.

'Yes, go and make yourself useful, Cary,' his grandmother agreed, which once again caused him some irritation, Juliet could see. 'And bring a fresh pot of coffee when you come back. It will save Josie's legs.'

'I'm not a servant, Grandmama.'

For once he seemed prepared to stick up for himself, but Lady Elinor soon put him straight. 'Nor is Josie,' she retorted, waving her cane like a magic wand. 'Off you go. And don't be too long.'

To Juliet's amazement, Cary didn't argue. He merely inclined his head before walking meekly to the door. It astonished her that he'd let the old lady walk all over him. Was he prepared to take any amount of humiliation just to ensure his inheritance? It seemed so.

'And did you enjoy your walk?' asked Lady Elinor as soon as Cary was out of earshot, and Juliet nodded.

'Very much.'

'Where did you go? Along the river bank? Didn't Josie warn you it's very wet at this time of year?'

'Um—Mr Marchese did, actually.'

'Rafe?' The old lady frowned. 'Rafe was here?'

Juliet felt the colour entering her cheeks. 'Yes. I think he brought some—things—for Mrs Morgan. I was up early and I happened to be in the kitchen when he arrived.'

'Ah.' Lady Elinor looked thoughtful. 'So—what is your opinion of Rafe?'

'Oh…' Juliet was nonplussed. She didn't even want to think about Cary's cousin. 'He—er—he seems very nice. Does he live near here?'

Lady Elinor gave a short laugh. 'My dear, there is nothing remotely nice about my eldest grandson. Aggravating, provocative, fascinating, even. But not *nice*. That is such a namby-pamby word.'

Juliet pressed her lips together. 'He's—not much like Cary, is he?'

'No. Thank God!' The old lady reached for her cup of coffee and took a drink before continuing, 'So—I gather Rafe didn't tell you where he lives.'

'No.' Juliet shook her head. And then, wanting to explain herself, 'We didn't talk for long.'

'Well, he lives in Polgellin Bay. Above his studio, actually. Though he works at a school in Bodmin, as I believe I told you before.'

Juliet nodded. Then, in an effort to keep the conversation moving, 'Do you have any of his paintings, Lady Elinor?'

There was silence for a short while and Juliet was beginning to wonder if she'd said the wrong thing, when the old lady answered her. 'Rafe doesn't believe I'm interested in his work,' she said, somewhat obliquely. 'But I'd be interested to hear your opinion, Juliet.'

Like that was going to happen, thought Juliet wryly. Even if Rafe's studio were open to the public, that was the last place Cary would take her.

'Have you and Cary set a date for the wedding?'

The question was so unexpected after what they'd been discussing, Juliet was briefly at a loss for words. Then, 'Oh, no. We—er—we've just got engaged. We're not thinking of getting married for some time.'

'I thought not.'

The old lady's words were disturbing and, realising Cary wouldn't thank her if she created doubts in his grandmother's mind, Juliet hurried on. 'Maybe—maybe we'll think about it later in the year.'

'You're not wearing a ring.' Lady Elinor was far too shrewd not to have noticed.

'No.' Juliet had no answer for that either, and she wished Cary were here to share the grief.

'I imagine my grandson is fairly short of funds, as usual,' the old lady continued. 'Remind me to look in my jewellery box, Juliet. I may have just the ring for you to wear.'

Oh, God!

Juliet couldn't meet her eyes. This was so much worse than anything she could have anticipated. Imagining herself wearing a ring that Lady Elinor might once have worn when she was a young woman was mortifying. She'd never felt so despicable in her life.

It was hardly a relief to hear Cary coming back. The damage had been done, and there was no way her 'fiancé' was going to turn the old lady down. Indeed, as soon as they got back to London he'd probably take the ring and have it valued. If it was worth more than a few pounds, she doubted Lady Elinor would see it again.

Naturally, his grandmother told him of her suggestion. 'As I'm giving a small dinner party tomorrow evening to celebrate your engagement, I can hardly have Juliet turning up without an engagement ring, can I?'

'You're a brick, Grandmama!' exclaimed Cary at once, giving her an enthusiastic hug that almost caused Hitchins to renew hostilities. 'What would we do without you?'

# CHAPTER SIX

JULIET was getting ready for dinner when Josie tapped at her door.

At first she was tempted to ignore it, to pretend she hadn't heard the knock. She was uneasily aware that it could be Cary. And while he knew that her being here was simply as a favour to him—OK, he was paying her to pretend to be his fiancée, but that was all—no one else did. And she didn't altogether trust him not to try and take advantage of it. Particularly after what had happened that afternoon.

Juliet had hoped that Lady Elinor might forget about her offer to give her a ring. But, immediately after lunch, she'd asked Josie to bring her jewellery box and she'd spent the next half-hour poring over its contents.

Juliet had been aware that Cary had been dying to see what was in the velvet-lidded box his grandmother guarded so fiercely. But the old lady had made sure he was sitting at the opposite end of the table while she examined its contents. A man shouldn't be too curious, she'd told him. He'd see the rings she'd chosen for Juliet to choose from in the fullness of time.

Juliet herself hadn't wanted to have any part of it, but in that she'd had no choice. Even without Cary's arm lying possessively about her shoulders, Lady Elinor had expected her to be involved, and that was that.

The rings the old lady had eventually laid out on the crisp linen tablecloth sparkled in the sunlight. They were obviously very old, but remarkably contemporary in design. There was a diamond solitaire, an emerald dress ring, surrounded by rose-cut diamonds, and a single ruby, set in a circle of what Juliet suspected were semi-precious gems.

Juliet heard Cary's greedy intake of breath when he saw the rings. She was almost able to guess what he was thinking, could hear the calculator in his brain working out their exact value to him.

'Which do you find appealing, Juliet?' Lady Elinor asked, inviting her to sit beside her. 'As you can see, they're all practically antique. The diamond belonged to my grandmother, the emerald was a gift to my mother from the Brazilian cultural attaché, while the ruby was given to me when I was presented at court.'

Juliet shook her head. 'They're all very beautiful.'

'Yes, they are.' Cary spoke in her ear, apparently unable to resist joining them and picking up the diamond solitaire. She'd seen him pretending to admire the ring, when in actual fact he'd been assessing its potential. 'This is awfully kind of you, Grandmama. I know both Juliet and I are very grateful, aren't we, darling?'

Juliet's smile was forced as she looked up at him. 'Very,' she agreed through clenched teeth. Then she whisked the diamond out of his hand and set it back on the cloth. 'I don't know which to choose.'

'Oh, I think the solitaire is the most appropriate,' Cary declared tightly. 'It looks the most like an engagement ring to me.'

It would, Juliet thought scornfully, knowing exactly how his mind was working. 'Actually,' she said, picking up the ruby, 'I think this is the one I like best.'

'But—'

'I'm sure you'd agree that, as Juliet is going to wear the ring, she should be the one to make the decision,' his grandmother had interposed smoothly. 'I must say, I like the ruby myself. It's a Burmese stone and it's flawless.'

And small, Juliet had reflected gratefully before going for

her shower. She would not be a party to Cary's taking his grandmother for every penny he could get.

Now, hearing someone at the door, she wondered if he'd decided to challenge her on it. She knew he hadn't been pleased when they'd left the dining room but, pleading tiredness, she'd been able to avoid a confrontation. Almost two days over, she thought, wrapping her silk robe tightly about her. She just had to get over tomorrow and then they'd be heading home.

But there was still tonight and, pulling open the door, she prepared herself to face his wrath. After all, he'd had all afternoon to feed his resentment, and something told her Cary wasn't the type of man to forget a grievance.

So she was pleasantly surprised when she saw who her visitor was, even though Josie looked rather harassed. 'Oh, Miss Lawrence,' she said, apparently forgetting that Juliet had asked her to use her first name, 'I was beginning to think you and Mr Cary must have gone out.'

'Oh—no. I was just in the bathroom.' Juliet felt guilty now for keeping the old woman waiting. 'Is something wrong?'

'Well—just a hiccough.'

Josie was decidedly flustered, and although Juliet suspected she wouldn't take her up on it she invited the housekeeper into the room and offered her a seat. In fact, the woman seemed grateful for her consideration, perching on a chair by the door and twisting her hands together in her lap.

'It's just—well, Lady Elinor won't be joining you for dinner this evening,' she said. 'She's not at all well. I've had to call Dr Charteris.'

Juliet was genuinely concerned. 'Is there anything I can do?'

'I doubt it.' Josie pulled a face. 'She hates being incapacitated. And she wouldn't thank you for visiting her right now, I can tell you. She's not going to be pleased with me when she hears I've called the doctor as it is.'

'But, if she's not well—'

'I know.' Josie grimaced. 'But that's the way she is.' She

paused. 'Anyway, I was wondering whether you and Mr Cary would mind having a cold meal this evening? What with the doctor coming and all—'

'Of course.' Juliet couldn't let her go on. 'Don't worry about us, Mrs Morgan. A sandwich would do.'

'Oh, I don't think Mr Cary would agree—'

'I'll make sure that Mr Cary agrees,' Juliet assured her firmly, ignoring the fact that only minutes before she'd been feeling apprehensive of seeing him again. 'Perhaps I could help you?'

Josie looked at her, wide-eyed. 'I don't think Lady Elinor would approve of that.'

'Lady Elinor doesn't need to know, does she?' Juliet smiled encouragingly. 'Actually, I'd enjoy it.'

Josie got to her feet again. 'I don't know what to say, Miss Lawrence.'

'You can start by calling me Juliet,' Juliet told her firmly. 'Now—when is the doctor due?'

About three-quarters of an hour later, Juliet was in the kitchen grating cheese when Cary put his head round the door.

'Oh, there you are!' he exclaimed, not noticing what she was doing for a moment. 'You must be the most elusive woman I've ever met. You're always disappearing somewh— What the hell are you doing?'

Juliet put down the grater. 'What does it look like I'm doing?'

'It looks as if you're doing Josie's job,' he retorted coldly. 'Where is she? Wasting time, as usual?'

'I don't think Josie has any time to waste,' said Juliet tersely. 'Have you any idea how much work is entailed in running a place like this? No, I thought not.'

Cary scowled. 'I still don't understand what you're doing here. Do you want the old girl to think I'm marrying a scrubber?'

Juliet caught her breath. 'No one's likely to think that but you, Cary. And what's wrong with being a scrubber anyway? It's a job of work, isn't it, and in my situation beggars can't be choosers.'

'Oh, come off it. You wouldn't dream of cleaning people's houses for a living. And, besides, it's only an expression. What I really meant was, I don't think Grandmama would approve of her guest preparing her own dinner.'

'Your grandmother isn't well,' said Juliet shortly. 'Didn't Josie tell you? She's had to call the doctor.'

'Charteris.' Cary said the man's name almost consideringly. Then, 'No sweat! But no. No one told me anything.'

Juliet frowned, suddenly noticing that Cary was still wearing the grey trousers and tweed jacket he'd been wearing that afternoon. 'What have you been doing?'

'Oh…' Cary looked a little furtive now. 'This and that.' And then, as if he had something of importance to tell her, he let the door close behind him and came across to the table where she was working. 'Actually,' he went on in a low voice, 'I've been checking the books.'

'The books?' Juliet looked confused.

'The estate books,' whispered Cary, his excitement barely controlled. 'God, you'll never believe what I found!'

Distaste showed on Juliet's face, but she couldn't help the obvious question, 'Did your grandmother ask you to look at them?'

'The old girl?' Cary scoffed. 'Not likely.'

'So she doesn't know what you've been doing?'

'No.' Cary was impatient. 'But never mind that now, I saw this letter—'

'I don't think you should be reading your grandmother's correspondence,' said Juliet severely. 'Her letters are private.'

'Oh, for pity's sake.' Cary snorted. 'She lets that bastard, Marchese, keep her accounts.'

'Don't call him that.'

'Oh, hello, are you a fan of his, too?'

'No.' But Juliet knew she'd gone red. 'I just don't think you should call him that.'

'Yeah, right.' Cary was scornful. 'Anyway, forget about him. The old girl's had an offer for Tregellin. Can you believe that?

I doubt if even that—Marchese knows about it. Some property developer from Bristol wants to buy the house, the farms, everything. He wants to build an estate of luxury homes on the site, with a golf course, clubhouse, the whole works. The offer's probably worth millions!'

Juliet stared at him in dismay. 'You're not serious!'

'I am.'

'I can't believe that Lady Elinor would consider selling out to a developer.'

'Well, of course she wouldn't!' exclaimed Cary irritably. 'That's why I've never heard about it. The offer was made months ago. My guess is, she rejected it outright.'

'Thank goodness.'

Juliet's response was heartfelt. She might have only been here a couple of days, but she already cared about the place. The house might need renovating and she was sure it fairly devoured the cash for its upkeep, but its position was incomparable. She shuddered at the thought of a string of wealthy investors buying second homes on the land where the house and grounds used to be, polluting the air with their gas-guzzling cars and frightening the birds away.

'What do you mean, thank goodness?' Cary was impatient. 'It's the chance of a lifetime. I wouldn't turn it down. I'd grab it with both hands.'

'Which is probably why you haven't heard about it.' Juliet was scathing. 'And you haven't even asked how your grandmother is. She could be dying for all you know.'

'No such luck,' muttered Cary, barely audibly, but Juliet heard him and her lip curled in contempt. 'Anyway, what are you doing?' he demanded, changing the subject. 'Playing housemaid?'

'I'm helping Josie,' retorted Juliet, returning to her grating. 'With your grandmother being unwell, she asked if we'd mind having a cold meal tonight, but I thought I might improve on that. What do you think?'

'You're making the meal?' Cary was aghast. 'You're not a cook!'

'No.' Juliet conceded the fact. 'But I found some kidneys in the fridge and I'm planning on sautéing them with some bacon. I thought we might have baked potatoes, too, topped with grated cheese. Does that sound good to you?'

Cary grimaced. 'Kidneys! I don't eat offal!'

You would if your grandmother offered it, thought Juliet irritably, but she held her tongue. 'So—you'll have sandwiches, right?'

'Sandwiches!' Cary gave her a scornful look. 'You have got to be joking.' He paused. 'How about going out?'

'Going out?'

'Yeah. We could go into Bodmin, meet up with some friends of mine, find a club, get something to eat there. They might even have a casino. What about it?'

'What about your grandmother?'

'Oh, please.' Cary groaned. 'She won't want to see me.' Then he frowned. 'Where's your ring?'

'In my pocket.' She was wearing navy linen trousers this evening with a warm pink angora sweater, whose V neckline was lower than she could have wished. She shook her head. 'Don't you ever think about anything else but money?'

'Give me a break.' Cary turned towards the door. 'So that's a no, is it? You're not coming?'

'Correct.'

Juliet refused to look at him, and with a grunt of resignation he left the kitchen. She half hoped he might change his mind and go and see his grandmother, but a few minutes later she heard the sound of a car being started and then the distant roar of the engine as he drove away.

Dammit!

She didn't usually swear, but Cary's selfishness really got to her. She wanted to put down the grater and abandon any attempt at making a meal.

But a few minutes later, when Josie came into the room, the

smell of cooking food had her wrinkling her nose with pleasure. 'Oh, Miss—Juliet—you didn't have to do this.'

'Why not?' Juliet smiled at her. 'I imagine Lady Elinor can eat something, can't she? Kidneys are supposed to be good for the digestion, I believe.'

Josie came to squeeze her arm. 'You're a kind girl,' she said fiercely. 'Who'd have thought Mr Cary would find himself a nice girl like you?'

'Who'd have thought it?' agreed Juliet drily, but she kept her real feelings to herself.

With Josie's approval, Juliet ate her supper in the conservatory. She did consider taking her tray upstairs, but now that Cary had gone out she felt more at ease and the conservatory was still warm after being bathed in sunshine for most of the day.

She was pushing a slightly burned kidney round her plate when she became aware that she had company. The conservatory was lit by patio lights, only a couple of which were actually illuminated, and she got quite a start when she saw a tall dark figure standing in the doorway to the morning room.

'Hi,' said her visitor, making no attempt to come further into the room. 'Josie said I'd find you here.'

Juliet took a steadying breath. 'Were you looking for me?'

'I came to see the old lady,' Rafe corrected her drily. 'Josie rang and told me she'd called the doctor.'

'Ah.' Juliet nodded. Despite her reservations about him, she was fairly sure that Rafe thought more of his grandmother than Cary ever had. 'So—how is she tonight?'

'Frustrated.' Rafe propped a shoulder against the frame of the door. 'She dislikes having Charteris telling her to look after herself.'

'But she should.' Juliet didn't know whether to get to her feet or stay where she was. 'And if there's anything I can do to help…'

Rafe inclined his head. He was wearing black pleated trousers this evening and a white silk shirt. The cuffs of his shirt were rolled back to his elbows, and her eyes were drawn to the contrast between the fabric and the dark tan of his skin. She wondered if he'd been planning on going out when Josie phoned. Whether he'd had a date with some young woman he was interested in.

'In the normal way, she doesn't have a problem,' Rafe said at last, aware that his own motive for coming to find Juliet was hardly commendable. When the old lady had told him what had happened, that their visitor had made a meal for them all, he'd felt a compelling desire to thank her. But now, standing here, looking at the attractive picture she made in the lamplight, he wondered if gratitude had really been at the top of his list.

'You mean you think our being here might be too much for her?' Juliet had interpreted his words to mean that she and Cary were the real reason Lady Elinor had had to take to her bed.

'No.' Rafe shook his head. 'She had a bad dose of flu in February. Charteris warned her to take things easy for a while, but you must have realised by now that the old lady doesn't play by anyone's rules but her own.'

Juliet frowned. 'Are you worried about her?'

'No more than usual.' Rafe's tone was dry. 'By the way, she asked me to tell you, the kidneys were delicious.'

Juliet's cheeks turned a becoming shade of pink. 'She didn't really say that.'

'She did.' Rafe hesitated a moment and then left the door and walked slowly across the tiled floor. He knew he was tempting the devil by being here, but Josie had also told him that Cary had gone out and he enjoyed baiting his fiancée. She was such an easy target. 'So where's the boy wonder this evening?' he asked casually, pausing beside her chair. 'Checking out the local talent?'

'No!' Juliet had hoped they could have a conversation without resorting to sarcasm. 'He's gone into Bodmin to meet some friends, I believe. If it's any business of yours.'

Rafe dropped down into the chair opposite her, and she immediately felt as if the room was too small. Or perhaps it was just that he was too close, the cooling atmosphere in the conservatory making her overly aware of his heat.

'So why didn't you go with him?' he asked, spreading his thighs and allowing his hands to hang loosely between his knees. 'Or didn't he ask you?'

'He asked me!' Juliet was defensive, even though she was telling the truth. 'I didn't want to go out.'

Rafe's dark brows formed a V, but he didn't argue with her. Instead he contented himself with just looking at her, apparently waiting for her to say something else. He had the unnerving ability to create tension between them when she had no earthly reason to be apprehensive of him. Heavens, she'd hoped this morning that he was beginning to accept her, but now she sensed another attitude entirely.

And, thinking of the morning, she finally thought of something she could say. 'I—er—I enjoyed my walk,' she said, trying to control the breathy element in her voice. 'This morning, I mean. And—and you were right about it being wet. Without Mrs Morgan's boots, my feet would have been soaked to the skin.'

Rafe's eyes narrowed on her suddenly animated face. He knew she was nervous of him. He'd sensed that from the first time he'd met her, but he couldn't decide whether it was a sexual awareness or something else. One thing was certain—she didn't act like any divorced woman he'd ever known. She seemed far too innocent in his opinion, although again he could be wrong. It might all be an act gauged to arouse his sympathy. Despite his reservations, he was tempted to find out.

'How long have you and Cary been engaged?' he asked, without warning, and Juliet looked momentarily like a rabbit caught in the headlights of his car.

'Um—a few weeks,' she said vaguely. Then, as if inspired, 'We've known one another since we were children.'

'Yeah, I know that.' Rafe smoothed one lean brown hand over his knee. 'The old lady told me.'

'Lady Elinor tells you a lot.'

The words were out before she could prevent them and Rafe gave her a wry smile before saying, 'Does that bother you?'

'Of course not.' Juliet swallowed. 'Obviously, you're very close to her.'

Rafe shook his head. 'I doubt if the old lady is close to anyone. Except Josie, maybe.'

'That's not true.'

'You don't think she's close to Cary, do you?'

'He's her grandson.' Juliet was defensive again.

'He's also a selfish creep. Even you must know that.'

Juliet's lips parted and she got jerkily to her feet. 'You have no right to say things like that to me!'

'No?' To her dismay, Rafe stood also, and although she was a tall girl, she still had to tilt her head to look up at him. 'You're not going to tell me that with your experience you can't recognise his faults? I thought they must be part of his charm.'

Juliet gasped. 'That's insulting!'

Rafe knew he had gone too far, but he couldn't seem to control this totally negative desire to provoke her. 'How have I insulted you? By assuming that, as you've been married before you must have some experience of men? Or by doubting Cary's charm?'

'You know what you said,' she retorted, stung into retaliation. 'Is that what you tell Lady Elinor? That—that Cary's a selfish—what you said?'

'A creep! I said he was a creep, and he is,' said Rafe harshly, but he was aware she'd scraped a nerve. 'And if you think I need to tell the old lady that, then you don't know her at all.'

'I don't.' But Juliet knew her words had been as unforgivable as his. However, she couldn't back down now. 'I don't know her or you,' she added tersely. 'If you'll excuse me, I'd like to take my tray back to the kitchen.'

'And if I won't? Excuse you, I mean?' Rafe stepped in front of the table where she'd left the remains of her meal. 'We haven't finished our conversation.'

'I have,' said Juliet, aware that the anger she'd summoned so bravely was rapidly draining away. She held up her head, though she avoided those dark, disturbing eyes. 'Why are you doing this, Mr Marchese? You don't even like me.'

Rafe almost gasped. 'I didn't say that.'

'You didn't have to.' Juliet decided to abandon her plan to return the tray, but she didn't feel she could just storm out of the room. 'If I've offended you, Mr Marchese, I'm sorry. For some reason, we seem to rub one another up the wrong way.'

Rafe wanted to groan with frustration. Her choice of words was so formal, so *prim*. God, he was the one who ought to retract his words. She was hopelessly inexperienced for her age. What kind of a man had she married? What kind of a marriage had it been?

Later on, he told himself he hadn't intended to touch her. He'd wanted to provoke her, yeah; to get her to shed that prissy way of talking to him and behave like any other woman of his acquaintance. But she was still Cary's fiancée, for pity's sake, and he had some sense of honour beneath the tough exterior he showed to the world. Besides, he'd never seduced another man's woman, and he'd had no intention of doing so now.

Yet he stopped her when she would have turned away from him, imprisoned her beside him with one slightly cruel hand about her wrist. And then, when she'd stared up at him with shocked, indignant eyes, he'd cupped her nape with his free hand and brought her mouth to his.

# CHAPTER SEVEN

JULIET huddled under the covers of her bed knowing she'd done something totally stupid. No matter how she tried to justify what had happened, nothing could alter the fact that she was supposed to be Cary's fiancée and she'd let Rafe Marchese kiss her.

*Kiss her!*

Was that really all he'd done? Was that a genuine description of his hungry possession of her mouth? Dear God, she felt as if he'd ravaged her. How else to explain the searching pressure of his tongue against her teeth, the pitiful defence she'd put up before she'd let him have his way with her?

Well, to be honest, he hadn't actually had his way with her, she reassured herself. He'd kissed her, yes; he'd thrust his tongue down her throat. He'd even pushed his leg between hers to bring her closer. But he hadn't actually touched her intimately. Not really. Even if she was still wet and throbbing from her own pathetic arousal.

How on earth had it happened? she asked herself for the umpteenth time. One minute she'd been preparing a dignified exit, and the next he'd grabbed her and pulled her into his arms. Why hadn't she stopped him? Why hadn't she slapped him or said something to wipe that predatory look off his face? Why had she behaved as if he held all the cards?

But, heavens, her limbs had turned to jelly as soon as he'd put his arms around her. He'd held her so close to him that she'd

felt the taut muscles of his thighs against her legs. Her breasts
had been crushed against his chest in a way that must have left
him in no doubt as to their reaction, and when his hand had
cupped her bottom she'd felt an unfamiliar wetness in her pants.

Touching her breasts now, she discovered they were still hot
and heavy. Much like his erection, she remembered, shivering
convulsively. He'd felt so big, so powerful, pushing against her
stomach with an insistence she'd never experienced before.
David had made love to her, but she'd never responded so violently. And, God help her, she'd wanted Rafe to show her exactly
how satisfying making love with him might be.

Which was unforgivable on all counts. What was wrong with
her, for goodness' sake? What had happened to the cool, controlled individual she'd always believed herself to be? Heavens,
she hadn't even caused a scene when David had walked out on
her. Was that because she'd felt she deserved it or because she
hadn't really cared?

And why was she having this crisis of identity now? Just
when she was supposed to behave with the style and confidence
for which she'd once been famous? What was it about Rafe
Marchese that made her act in a way that was totally unfamiliar to her? What she did know was that if Rafe had been the one
to ask her to *act* as his fiancée, she'd be in deep trouble now.

Even deeper than the trouble she was already in, she acknowledged. Dear heaven, the man had only kissed her and
already she was a quivering wreck.

Looking back, from the safety of her bed, Juliet wondered
now what might have happened if Josie hadn't interrupted them.
Fortunately they'd heard her footsteps as she crossed the hall,
and by the time she'd appeared in the doorway Rafe had put half
the width of the conservatory between them. But she was sure
he must have been glad of the comparative darkness to conceal
his frustration. Juliet knew she'd been flushed and breathless,
limp with relief or disappointment. She wasn't sure which.

\* \* \*

On Saturday morning, Cary suggested they take a trip into Polgellin Bay.

Juliet had no idea what time he'd returned the night before and she didn't really care, but she did think he ought to spend some time with his grandmother instead of going out again.

'Oh, she's OK,' he said when she broached the subject with him. 'I went to see her earlier on and she said she was feeling much better.'

Juliet wasn't sure whether this was the truth or not, but her own conscience was still pricking her and she didn't feel she had the right to criticise Cary's behaviour when her own was so much less than perfect. But she suspected his information had come from Josie. When she'd seen Lady Elinor earlier, she'd said nothing about her grandson. Only Rafe.

The old lady had sent word with Josie that she'd like to speak to Juliet after breakfast. She'd been eating in the dining room. Cary hadn't come down yet, and, although Juliet had offered to have her meal in the kitchen with the housekeeper, Josie had been adamant.

'We don't want you going away with the idea that a visit to Tregellin means doing for yourself,' she'd declared firmly. 'Now, you sit yourself at the table, and I'll fetch you some coffee and toast.'

It was when Josie came back to see if Juliet needed anything else that she delivered Lady Elinor's summons. 'She'll be getting up later on,' she confided, 'but I think she's concerned that you might feel you have to hang about here until she appears. She's feeling much better this morning. Quite looking forward to the dinner party tonight. Now, I'll show you to her room. She should have finished her breakfast by now.'

Lady Elinor lay propped on lace-edged pillows in a bed as big, if not bigger, than the one Juliet had slept in. Her room was huge, too, with the kind of antique furniture Juliet had only ever seen in a saleroom. But for all its faded grandeur, there was something impressive about it, and the view from the windows was worth a king's ransom.

Or a developer's fortune, thought Juliet unwillingly, remembering what Cary had told her. If she were Lady Elinor, she'd do everything she could to hang on to this place. It wasn't just a house. It was a family tradition.

'You saw Rafe last night.'

After giving an impatient response to Juliet's concerned questions about her health, Lady Elinor got straight to the point.

'Um—yes.' Juliet hoped her face wasn't as revealing as her uncertain stomach. Already the coffee she'd had for breakfast was threatening to return. 'I believe you spoke to him, too.'

'Well, of course. He came to see me.' The old lady was complacent. 'He worries about me. Or so he says.'

'I'm sure we were all concerned about you yesterday evening,' said Juliet carefully. Dammit, she owed Cary her support. 'Rafe—Rafe said you'd had flu earlier in the year and perhaps you were doing too much.'

'Rafe should keep his opinions to himself,' retorted Lady Elinor shortly. 'Who was it that called Charteris? Was it him?'

'No, I think that was Josie,' said Juliet, hoping she wasn't treading on anyone's toes. Then, appealingly, 'It's always best to have a professional judgement.'

'Humph.' The old lady regarded her dourly. 'It comes to something when you can't make a decision for yourself.' She frowned and then changed the subject entirely. 'Did you tell Rafe I'd given you a ring?'

Juliet caught her breath. 'No.'

'Why not?' She frowned. 'I'm surprised he didn't ask you about it.'

Juliet moistened her lips. 'Well, actually, I wasn't wearing it.' She paused and when it became apparent that something more was required, she added awkwardly, 'I'd put it in my pocket while I was helping Mrs Morgan prepare supper, and I'm afraid I forgot about it. Until—until later.'

Until she'd escaped from the conservatory, actually. Uneasily she remembered running up the stairs, scolding herself for what had happened, feeling like a scarlet woman. She'd pulled the ring out of her pocket then and rammed it onto her finger. As if it might act as some kind of talisman and erase the mistakes she'd made.

It hadn't, of course. But its glowing heart had sobered her. Reminded her that whatever happened here, she was not at all what either Rafe—or Lady Elinor—believed her to be.

'I see.' If she hadn't been feeling so ashamed, Juliet might have wondered at the faintly smug gleam that entered the old lady's eyes at her words. 'Well, you're wearing it this morning.'

'Oh—yes.' Juliet couldn't prevent the index finger of her right hand from circling the flawless stone. 'It's so beautiful! Naturally I'll give it back before we leave.'

'Give it back?' Lady Elinor stared at her disapprovingly. 'Of course you won't give it back. The ring is yours.'

'But—' The words stuck in her throat but Juliet knew she had to say them. 'If—when—Cary buys me an engagement ring, I won't need it any more.'

'You don't like it?'

'Of course I like it.'

'Then we'll hear no more about it.' The old lady flapped a dismissive hand. 'It pleases me to think that my grandson's wife will wear the ring. That in time she'll pass it on to her granddaughter. Now, I don't want you spending the day worrying about me. Get out and enjoy yourselves. I'll see you later.'

And that was how Juliet had had to leave it. But she wasn't happy about the situation and she determined that when her 'engagement' to Cary ended, she'd return the ring to Lady Elinor with her gratitude.

Now, aware that Cary was still waiting for an answer to his invitation, Juliet gave in. If they were out of the house for a few hours, Lady Elinor would have time to get more rest. Besides, she would enjoy seeing a little more of the surrounding area. So far, apart from her walk along the river bank, she'd spent all her time in the house.

Telling Josie what they were doing, they left Tregellin a few minutes later. It was already after ten o'clock and, although it had rained earlier, a watery sun was breaking through the clouds as they drove down the valley towards the coast. The road twisted and turned, high hedges giving glimpses of the sea in places, the salty breeze blowing strongly from the west.

Polgellin Bay was bigger than Juliet had expected. They'd followed the coastal road into the resort, passing pretty villas with palm trees growing in their back gardens, the lushness of the vegetation an indication of how temperate the climate must be. A narrow main street angled down to a harbour, with fishing boats and fancy yachts protected by a sea wall.

Cary parked by the harbour. At this time of year it was nowhere near as busy as it would be in the season, he told her. At present, it was possible to walk into the shops and cafés without difficulty. In late spring and early summer, the crowds made getting around at all a nightmare.

Juliet doubted anywhere so pretty could be deemed a nightmare whatever the season. Now that the sun had come out it was quite warm, and she was glad she'd shed her jeans in favour of low-rise cotton trousers. Teamed with a hot-pink camisole and a white cotton shirt, they made her feel as if she was on holiday. Maybe for a few hours she could forget the duplicity of her role.

A harbourside pub offered outdoor tables, and Cary suggested they have a drink before going to explore the town. 'Just coffee for me,' said Juliet firmly, but she appreciated the opportunity to sit and enjoy the activity around them. A fishing boat had just come in and she could see dark grey lobsters and wriggling crabs being tossed into an ice-filled trough.

Afterwards, they strolled up the steep street they'd driven down earlier. Many shops with famous names vied with local dealers for trade. There were numerous cafés and lots of gift shops, as well as several art galleries, with canny stacks of posters outside to lure the customers in.

Juliet found herself saying, 'This is where—your cousin has his studio, isn't it?' and then cursed her impulsive tongue when Cary gave her a knowing look.

'Yeah,' he said flatly. 'Well, not here, exactly. It's up one of these side-streets. He can't afford the rents on these premises with what he makes from his daubings.'

Juliet sucked in a breath. 'I gather you're not interested in art.'

Cary snorted. 'Art, yes. What he produces, no.' He sneered when he saw how his contemptuous words had affected her. 'Come on, then. I'll show you. I'm sure Rafe won't turn you away.'

'Oh—no…'

The last thing Juliet wanted was to see Rafe this morning. Dear lord, he was going to think she'd arranged this outing. That, in spite of the way she'd scuttled away last night, she couldn't wait to see him again. Which was patently untrue, she told herself, as Cary took her arm to guide her up another steep street running parallel with the harbour. Indeed, she'd been hoping she wouldn't see him again before they left.

'Honestly, I don't think this is a good idea,' she protested, pulling herself free of his hand and surreptitiously wiping her damp palms on her trousers. 'The studio may be closed.'

'It may,' agreed Cary without sympathy. 'But I'll get him to open it up. He just lives over the place, after all, and he's not likely to be teaching on Saturday.'

The door to the studio was closed and blinds were half-drawn against the glare of the sun. There didn't seem to be anybody about and Juliet was about to suggest that they should leave it when a woman got out of a sleek Mercedes coupé across the street and walked towards them.

'Are you looking for Rafe?' she asked, with the kind of confidence that could only come from knowing him well. 'Hey, you're his cousin, aren't you?' she went on, staring at Cary. 'I remember seeing you around when you lived at Tregellin.'

Juliet saw at once that Cary didn't like being associated with Rafe. And, from his expression, he didn't care for her familiarity either. Though, looking at her deep cleavage and short pleated skirt, Juliet guessed she was just the sort of woman he usually preferred.

'I'm Cary Daniels, yes,' he said at last, realising he couldn't ignore her. Not in Juliet's presence, anyway. 'And you are?'

'Liv. Liv Holderness. Well, Liv Melrose, don't you remember? As I recall it, you used to be quite a regular at my dad's hotel.'

'My God!' Cary looked stunned. 'You're *Lady* Holderness?'

'One and the same,' agreed the woman nonchalantly. 'Bobby and I are having dinner with you and your grandmother this evening. Didn't she tell you?'

'I— She may have done.' Cary was clearly finding it difficult to come to terms with this development and Juliet wondered if his relationship with the woman had been as casual as he'd obviously like to pretend. He licked his lips. 'Are you here to see— Rafe?'

'That's for me to know and you to find out,' she declared playfully. Her gaze drifted over Juliet with a calculated interest. 'Who's this? Another relation?'

'Er—this is Juliet Lawrence. My fiancée,' said Cary swiftly, and Juliet saw the way Liv Holderness' eyes widened.

'Your fiancée?' she echoed, a faint smile hovering about her full lips. 'I bet your grandmother approves.'

'She does.' Juliet was stung into answering for herself. Then she looked at Cary. 'We ought to be going.'

'You've seen Rafe?'

The woman arched narrow brows, and Juliet knew an uncharacteristic urge to make some scathing comment about his choice of visitor. But, of course, she didn't, and it was left to Cary to admit that no, the studio didn't appear to be open.

'Well, it won't be,' said Liv Holderness impatiently. 'Rafe never works with an audience. Besides, he's probably up in his apartment. Have you rung the bell?'

'No.' Cary cast Juliet a helpless glance and then watched as the woman brushed past them and pressed a scarlet-tipped finger to the bell-push beside a painted door that hadn't seemed to Juliet to have any obvious connection to the studio. 'I didn't think he'd be in.'

Which was so patently untrue that Juliet could only stare at him in disbelief.

'Oh, he will be,' asserted Liv Holderness confidently. 'He's expecting me.'

Juliet's mouth was dry and she looked longingly over the rooftops towards the harbour. She so much didn't want to be here. Particularly not now she'd discovered that Rafe was apparently having some sort of relationship with this woman. Heavens, what was he going to think? That they were spying on him?

But it was too late. The door was swinging open and Rafe appeared, dark and disturbingly male in a cotton T-shirt and khaki shorts. He was wearing trainers, too, and, judging by the V of sweat that stained the front of his sleeveless T-shirt—and outlined every taut muscle—he'd either been running or doing some other physical exercise. And Juliet, who'd always believed she didn't like men in shorts, realised her opinion had been vastly under-researched.

'Darling!' Liv Holderness wrinkled her nose at him. 'What have you been doing?'

Rafe's expression mirrored his frustration. For God's sake, he thought, what the hell was Cary doing here? And Juliet. He'd have expected her to steer well clear of him from now on.

'You're early,' was all he said, totally ignoring his cousin's scornful face. 'I was just about to have a shower.'

'Not before time, I'd say,' declared Cary, giving Juliet a sardonic look. 'I didn't know splashing a paintbrush around could bring you out in a sweat!'

Juliet wanted to die with embarrassment, but Rafe just pulled a wry face. 'How would you know, Cary?' he enquired mockingly. 'I doubt if you've ever broken sweat in your life! Oh, except when the South African authorities were on your tail. I bet you weren't so smug then.'

'Why, you—'

Juliet didn't know what Cary might have done if Liv Holderness hadn't stepped forward at that moment. But whatever it was, she doubted her 'fiancé' would have come off the winner. Seeing them close together only made the difference between the two men so much sharper. The terrier and the tiger, she thought fancifully. There'd be no contest.

'Can we come up?'

It was the other woman who spoke and Juliet put a hand on Cary's arm, urging him to make some excuse for them to leave. But for some reason Cary wouldn't respond to her silent pleas. 'Yeah, how about it, Marchese?' he said. Then, in an aside to Juliet, 'I want to see where he lives. I bet it's a dump!'

Rafe wanted to refuse. Apart from the fact that he objected to spending any more time with Cary than he had to, he didn't want Juliet invading his space. She'd already invaded far more of his thoughts than was sensible in the circumstances. Dammit, she was his idiot cousin's fiancée. He had no right to be remembering how soft and responsive her mouth had been when he'd kissed her.

But Liv was no fool, he knew, and she'd soon suspect something was up if he acted out of character. So, with a gesture of resignation, he said, 'Yeah, come on up. Liv, you can make us some coffee.'

Juliet glared at Cary, but he only urged her forward. 'Hurry up, baby,' he said. 'You know you wanted to see where the great painter lived.'

If Rafe heard, he ignored it, and, cursing herself for creating this situation in the first place, Juliet followed Liv Holderness up a narrow flight of stairs. The other woman was wearing high heels and wobbled precariously on the worn treads. Juliet thought cynically that Cary's eyes were probably glued to the hem of the other woman's skirt which bobbed provocatively near the apex of her thighs.

The apartment they entered was surprisingly spacious. Or at least the living room was, Juliet amended, unable to deny her interest as she looked around. Compared to Tregellin, it was intensely modern, with an arrangement of chocolate brown leather sofas and armchairs at one end of the room and a wrought-iron dining set at the other. There was a comprehensive entertainment centre enclosed within a teak console and the positioning of various vases and small sculptures gave the room an elegant appearance. More elegant than Cary had expected, Juliet suspected, aware of his eyes assessing the room's tasteful appointments. Probably estimating how much they were worth, she thought, her cynicism asserting itself again, and she determinedly looked away.

And met their host's dark appraising gaze. She stiffened, almost instinctively, wondering if he intended to get his own back by mentioning their encounter the night before. But all he said was, 'If you'll excuse me…' and headed lazily towards an inner door that evidently led to the bathroom.

# CHAPTER EIGHT

OR HIS bedroom, Juliet reflected tensely, looking anywhere but into those magnetic eyes. But when he turned away she couldn't prevent herself from watching him, her gaze drawn to his tight buttocks and the hairy length of those long, powerful legs.

She swallowed and then became aware that her interest hadn't gone unnoticed. Cary was looking at her now with a mocking, speculative stare. Oh, God, she thought, how had she got herself into this situation? If Cary thought she was attracted to Rafe, heaven knew what mischief he might do.

Liv Holderness, meanwhile, had teetered her way across to where a breakfast bar hid a small kitchen. Limed-oak units with granite working surfaces gave the place a sophisticated look. There were spotlights in the ceiling and copper-bottomed pans hanging below wall cupboards, with earthenware bowls on the window sill, where spider ferns and other greenery tumbled to the floor.

Liv was obviously familiar with the kitchen's layout because she found the coffee-maker and grains without much effort. Juliet tried not to let her own feelings about Rafe impinge on her opinion of the woman, but the image of them together—in his bed—kept popping into her mind.

'Have you known Cary long?' Liv asked, and Juliet guessed she was trying to define their relationship. She didn't fool herself that the woman considered her any competition. Why should she? But she wanted to know what she was dealing with; if Rafe was involved.

'Since we were kids,' replied Cary at once, turning from the painting he'd been studying. 'So, what's going on with you and Marchese? Or is that a leading question?'

She smiled, but it didn't quite reach her eyes. 'I think that's our business, don't you?' Then she turned to Juliet. 'So what do you do when you're not spending time with Lady Elinor?'

Juliet swallowed, wishing Cary would answer that, too. To avoid doing so, she gestured towards a group of four water colours that hung on the wall beside the dining table. 'Is this Mr Marchese's work, Lady Holderness?'

'Call her Liv, for God's sake!' Cary scowled and the woman came out from behind the breakfast bar and gave Juliet a considering look.

'As if Rafe would hang anything of his in his apartment!' she exclaimed scornfully. 'No, these are Susie Rivers. She's what you might call a protégée of his.'

'He has a lot of them,' remarked Cary slyly, earning another acrimonious glare from Liv. He put his arm around Juliet, ignoring her resistance. 'Let's sit down, darling. I'm sure Rafe will be only too happy to show you his work, when he's cleaned up.'

To Juliet's relief, there were no more questions about her background and when Rafe came back into the room, they were all sitting down, drinking the coffee Liv Holderness had made. There were specks of water sparkling on his night-dark hair, a dark blue shirt and tight jeans accentuating his lean, muscled frame. He was barefoot, and in those first few seconds Juliet felt as if she knew everything about him. Well, about his appearance, anyway, she amended, wondering what it was about him that disturbed her so much.

'I'll get you a cup,' said Liv at once, but before she could get up Rafe waved her back into her seat.

'I can do it,' he said, going to pour himself some coffee.

Then, coming round the bar, he rested his hips against the granite counter. 'I'm so glad you've made yourselves at home.'

'No, you're not.' Liv was sardonic. 'I know you prefer your privacy when you're working.'

'I hope you don't expect us to believe he'd been working earlier,' Cary admonished. 'For heaven's sake, we're not morons.'

Rafe was tempted to make some cutting comment, but Juliet would be bound to get the wrong impression if he did. Just because he'd had a crisis of some sort the night before didn't mean he wanted to repeat the exercise.

'I'd been running,' he said, by way of an answer. 'I'm sorry if my appearance offended your sensibilities, Cary, but some of us get off our backsides from time to time.'

'Makes a change from crawling, I suppose,' retorted Cary derisively, and Juliet stifled a groan. For pity's sake, did he want to start a fight with the other man? She could sense the cold hostility in Rafe's narrow-eyed gaze.

'Just shut the hell up, will you, Cary?' Liv had evidently come to the same conclusion, but, unlike Juliet, she wasn't afraid to speak her mind.

'Who do you think you're talking to?' demanded Cary at once, but Liv wasn't listening to him. Instead she turned to Rafe again, her smile warm and familiar.

'I think Juliet wants to see some of your work, darling,' she said, as if Juliet was incapable of speaking for herself. 'Would you like me to take her down to the studio? Then you can finish your coffee in peace.'

'I don't think—' Juliet was beginning, when Rafe put down his cup.

'If Juliet wants to see the studio, I'll show it to her,' he said flatly. 'Is that what you want?' He looked directly at her. 'Make up your mind. I've got work to do.'

Juliet could hear Cary muttering about ignorant bastards and knew that any moment he was going to make some other remark that would further sour Rafe's mood. And, although she told herself that the last thing she wanted to do was be alone with him, what could it harm to see his studio and the work he was doing?

'Um—yes, I'd like that,' she said, ignoring Cary's outraged expression. 'Thanks.'

'I'll come with you,' said Liv at once, swallowing the last of her coffee and getting to her feet, and Rafe sighed. He guessed that if Liv accompanied them, Cary would, too, and he didn't want his cousin anywhere near his studio at present.

'The place isn't big enough for all of us,' he said, regarding her warningly. 'I've got work in progress that I don't want anyone else to see yet.'

'Oh…'

She got the message at once, he saw. Letting Cary see the sketches Rafe had been making for her portrait wasn't the wisest thing to do in the circumstances. It would be like him to drop that tasty little morsel into the conversation at dinner that evening and then pretend to be mortified when her husband expressed his surprise.

'Well—OK,' she said, and Juliet stared at her. Why had she suddenly changed her mind? 'Cary and I will have another cup of coffee. We can reminisce about old times.'

Cary wasn't at all suited. 'I didn't come to Polgellin Bay to sit in this apartment drinking coffee,' he grumbled, but Liv put on her most persuasive expression.

'Just for five more minutes,' she cajoled appealing. 'You can tell me what you've been doing since you left Tregellin.'

She'd taken hold of his arm now, and Juliet couldn't decide whether he was disgruntled or flattered. Either way, Rafe ushered her towards the door and other considerations took the place of curiosity.

There were two doors at the foot of the flight of stairs that led up to Rafe's apartment. One to the outdoors, she knew, and the other led into his studio. Rafe went ahead of her, switching on a couple of spotlights to illuminate an area bigger than she'd expected from what he'd said to Cary. But she didn't really blame him for not wanting his cousin to join them. They weren't exactly the best of friends.

The door closed behind her and Juliet struggled to concentrate on why she'd come here. She and Rafe were alone, it was true, but she didn't kid herself that this had been his idea. On the contrary, as he lifted a canvas off an easel that had been set up to one side of the studio, and stowed it at the back of the studio, she guessed he didn't want her to see his 'work-in-progress' either.

'It's very—impressive,' she said, looking about her. And it was certainly more professional than she'd imagined when Lady Elinor had spoken of it. Sketches littered a side-table and dozens of canvases were stacked against a wall. There were palette knives and brushes, drawing equipment, charcoal, chalk and varnish, as well as jars and jars of paint in every colour imaginable scattered about the floor.

'It's adequate,' he said, without pretension, turning to give her a narrow-eyed stare. 'But you didn't really want to see my work, did you?'

'Yes.' Juliet answered without thinking, unaware of how revealing her answer might sound. 'I really did. It's very—interesting.'

Damned with faint praise. Rafe's jaw compressed. 'If you say so.'

Juliet sighed. 'Why should it surprise you that I'd like to see your work? If you're thinking about what happened last night, forget it. I have.'

'It's good to know I'm so forgettable.'

Rafe spoke mockingly and Juliet wished she wasn't so aware of him in the confined space. The studio was filled with the mingled aromas of oil and other painting supplies, but she still couldn't ignore the subtle scent of man.

Licking her lips, she said, 'Do you want to talk about it? Is that what you're saying?'

Rafe made an indignant sound. 'Hey, you brought it up, not me.'

'I know I did, but—well, it shouldn't have happened. You know that as well as I do.' She glanced about her in an effort to change the subject. 'So may I see something?'

'Do you always switch from one thing to another like this?' His brows arched. 'I'm still trying to get my head round the fact that you didn't engineer this invitation just to spend some time alone with me.'

Juliet stared at him in frustration, the colour ebbing and flowing in her expressive face. 'Don't lie to me, Mr Marchese,' she said hotly. 'I'm engaged to Cary. That might not matter to you, but it matters to me.'

'Does it?' He couldn't prevent the amused retort. 'You know, I didn't get that impression last night.'

'No, well…' Juliet gave a careless shrug. 'You took me by surprise, that's all. I wasn't expecting it.'

'Believe it or not, neither was I,' remarked Rafe drily. Then, with cool deliberation, 'Did Cary tell you where he spent his evening? Did he meet up with the, in quotes, "friends" you spoke about?'

Juliet pursed her lips. 'I didn't ask him.'

'No?' Rafe couldn't help feeling pleased with her answer. 'Don't you care?'

Her colour deepened again. 'It's none of your business.'

'So—what are you saying? That you have an open relationship?' He paused and, when she didn't answer, he went on, 'That's when—'

'I know what an open relationship means,' she interrupted him fiercely. She wrapped her arms about herself. 'Can we talk about something else?'

'Your call.'

But he couldn't help wondering about her relationship with his cousin. Was she just humouring him until something better came along? It seemed likely, but he didn't care for the idea. And he despised himself for wanting something he couldn't—and shouldn't—have.

Forcing himself not to think about how her crossed arms pushed her small breasts into a prominent position, he abandoned his stance and walked across to where several canvases were propped against the brick wall. Swinging one around, he displayed a painting of an elderly fisherman sitting on a capstan by the harbour, his head bent over his nets.

Juliet, who'd been wishing she'd never come here, couldn't prevent an automatic gasp of admiration. 'Is this yours?' she asked, coming a little nearer and gazing raptly at the painting. 'My God, it's so lifelike! Is this a real person?'

'It was.' Rafe came to stand beside her, telling himself it was to get her perspective on the canvas. A faint scent came to his nostrils, warm and flowery and essentially feminine, like her. 'His name was John Tregaron. His family have lived in Polgellin for as long as anyone can remember.'

'That's amazing!'

'What? That his family have lived here for hundreds of years?'

Juliet gave him an impatient look and then wished she hadn't been so foolhardy when she met the disturbing darkness of his gaze. 'No,' she said, jerking her chin down again. 'You know what I mean. People must have complimented you on your work before.'

Rafe shrugged. 'Thank you.'

Juliet shifted a little uncomfortably. 'My father was a great admirer of certain painters' work. What little I know about art, I learned from him.'

Rafe wondered if she realised that was a double-edged comment. He guessed not. She was doing her best to normalise their relationship and he had to squash this unforgivable urge to bait her.

'I have my favourites, too,' he conceded, concentrating on the painting to avoid looking at her. 'When I was younger, I used to attend any exhibition I could get to. I started out by liking Turner and a contemporary of his, Thomas Girtin. Have you heard of him? Unfortunately he died when he was in his twenties. There's an anecdote about Turner saying that if Tom Girtin had lived, he'd have starved.'

'Do you believe that?'

Rafe shook his head. 'No, Turner was unique. But they did train together, and their earliest work was similar.'

Juliet was impressed and once again she made the mistake of looking up at him. But this time she couldn't look away. She was mesmerised by his eyes, by the sudden heat in his expression. She rubbed her elbows with her palms, trying to ignore the goose bumps that were feathering her skin.

This time, however, Rafe broke eye contact. Despite his determination not to pursue this unhealthy infatuation, there was an insistent hunger in his gut. He tried to tell himself it was because he hadn't had anything to eat before he went for his run, but his senses told him his need wasn't for food but something less admirable.

'Do—do you have anything else to show me?' Juliet ventured nervously, and Rafe ignored the innocent sexuality of her question and moved forward to replace the painting with a life-size sketch of Lady Elinor herself. It was roughly done, something he'd been working on without her knowledge. The old lady wouldn't sit for him. It would have smacked of giving him her approval.

'Oh—wow!' Juliet was entranced by his offering. 'I had no idea Lady Elinor had been here.'

'She hasn't.' Rafe's tone was flat. 'I did that from memory.'

'Well, it's very good.'

Rafe shrugged. 'I'm glad you approve.'

She smiled then, the corners of her mouth lifting to give her face a dangerous beauty. Dangerous, because she was such a temptation and she didn't know it.

'I approve of your work,' she said lightly. 'That's not to say I approve of you.'

'I'm wounded.' He paused, and then, as a thought occurred to him, 'Did your father approve of your husband?'

'My father?' She was taken aback. 'I— He never met David. He died soon after I left school.'

'I'm sorry.'

'Yes, so am I.' Juliet spoke philosophically. 'If he'd lived, I might not have made so many mistakes.'

Rafe hesitated. 'Because your marriage didn't work out?'

'You could say that.' Juliet pulled a face. 'He certainly wouldn't have trusted David with all *his* money.'

'You did that?'

It was a personal question but having come so far, Juliet couldn't back off. 'Yes,' she said, flushing with embarrassment. 'I know I was a fool. You can't despise me any more than I despise myself.'

'Why would I despise you?' Rafe was vehement. 'He sounds a complete bastard!'

Juliet grimaced. 'Tell me about it.'

'But charming, I guess. Was that why you married him?'

'I'm not sure why I married him now.' Juliet twisted her hands together at her waist. 'My father had just died and I have no brothers or sisters.' Then she broke off. 'But you don't want to hear this. I made a mistake. A lot of mistakes, actually. I'll get over it.'

Rafe half turned to look at her. 'And you think Cary's going to help you?'

Oh, God! Juliet closed her eyes for a moment. For a short while there, she'd actually forgotten why she was here. Thank goodness, she hadn't said anything too revealing. But it wasn't easy to lie, particularly to Rafe.

Which was another mistake.

'Um—I hope so,' she said now, trying to keep her voice light. 'Well, I don't have any money, so I can be sure he's not marrying me for that.'

'So why is he marrying you?' Rafe asked, unable to prevent himself, and Juliet caught her breath.

'Because he loves me, I suppose,' she said, wishing she sounded more convincing. 'Why don't you ask him?'

'I don't need to.' Rafe had reverted to sarcasm. 'Oh, Juliet, when will you ever learn?'

She gasped then. 'You know nothing about it.'

'Don't I?' His conviction disturbed her. 'I'd say I know Cary better than you do.'

'Oh, right.' Juliet knew she had to say something to defend herself. 'So when was the last time you slept with him? I'd be interested to know.'

Rafe scowled. 'I don't get into bed with reptiles.'

'Nor do I.' Juliet hated the smug look on his dark face. Their earlier civility seemed to have completely evaporated, and she despised herself anew for wishing things could be different. 'Besides,' she added, in an effort to be as objectionable as he was, 'I didn't think you were that choosy. Not judging by your current—what was it you called it—work-in-progress?'

Rafe was incensed. 'I hope you're not implying that I'm sleeping with Liv Holderness?'

'You're not?' Juliet managed to put just the right note of ridicule into her voice. 'Well, she wants you to. The woman can't take her eyes off your butt!'

Rafe's expression darkened with ominous intent, but then the humour of the situation brought an unwilling tilt to his lips. 'Now, I wonder why you noticed that,' he murmured softly. 'Isn't Cary enough for you?'

Her jaw dropped. 'That's a disgusting suggestion!'

Rafe was unrepentant, but he knew he'd already said more than he'd intended. All the same, it galled him that she couldn't see through Cary's lies. Dammit, the man was a walking contradiction.

Abandoning any thought of continuing their conversation, he went to restore the painting and the sketch of Lady Elinor to their original positions. He had to keep his mind on his work and nothing else, he warned himself. In another day or so she'd be gone.

Juliet, meanwhile, was fighting the urge to kick his provocative backside. He'd presented her with the perfect opportunity when he bent to straighten the canvases he'd moved earlier, his jeans outlining tight buttocks and long, powerful legs. Who did he think he was to speak to her like that? If it wasn't such a ludicrous notion, she'd have to wonder if he wanted her himself.

Which was so not true.

'I'm going back upstairs,' she said abruptly, deciding there was no point in trying to reason with him. 'I've seen all I came to see.'

Rafe turned, straightening. 'Well, that's something, I suppose.'

Juliet's lips tightened. 'You just love making fun of me, don't you?'

Rafe's mouth curled. 'Honey, you don't need me to do that,' he retorted harshly, before the reality of what he was saying occurred to him. But hell, she was too naïve for her own good and, if he didn't say anything, it was a fair bet that nobody else would. Particularly the old lady.

'You know—' her voice shook a little, but she carried on anyway '—you criticise Cary but, from where I'm standing, you're not so different.'

'Like hell!'

'I mean it.' She gained confidence from his angry rejoinder. 'You both think you know everything there is to know about women, but you don't.'

Rafe shook his head. 'Is that what you think this is about?'

She held up her head. 'Isn't it?'

'No.' He blew out a breath. 'Face it, Juliet, you know nothing about men. OK, you've been married and divorced and you should have gained some insight into the opposite sex, but you haven't. If you had, I wouldn't feel so bloody responsible.'

Juliet's eyes widened. 'There's no need for you to feel any responsibility towards me, Mr Marchese. I'm quite old enough to know what I'm doing, whatever you may think.'

'Yeah, right.'

He was dismissive and Juliet lost her temper. 'You know what I think, Mr Marchese?' she demanded. 'I think all this sanctimonious talk about responsibility is just a cover for what you really want.'

'Which is?' His tone was icy.

'The opportunity to oust Cary from his rightful place as your grandmother's legitimate heir,' she retorted recklessly and then almost collapsed with fear when his hand shot out and grabbed her wrist.

'Take that back,' he began grimly, but as she pressed her other hand to her throat, his expression grew even more menacing. *'Dios,'* he muttered, his eyes darkening until they were almost black. 'That ring!' He'd noticed her pretend-engagement ring, and now he reached out and pulled her hand towards him. 'Where did you get it?' he grated, his thumb pressing the stone painfully into her finger. 'Did Cary give it to you?'

Juliet swallowed, all her earlier bravado doused by the anguish in his face. 'I— Lady Elinor—g-gave it to me,' she stammered, his hard fingers burning into her flesh. She moistened dry lips. 'I've—I've only borrowed it.'

'Borrowed it?'

Rafe stared down at her with disbelieving eyes and she found herself stammering out an explanation even though he had no earthly right to expect one. 'We— Cary hasn't bought me a ring—yet,' she went on unsteadily. 'And your—your grandmother said that with the Holdernesses coming for dinner this evening I—I should be wearing one.'

'And she gave you this?' Rafe knew he shouldn't question the old lady's actions, but he couldn't deny the swirl of resentment that was building inside him.

'It's only borrowed,' Juliet said again, not understanding his attitude. But something was wrong here, and when she tried to pull away Rafe lifted her hand to study the glowing stone in closer detail.

'You really think Cary will allow you to return this?' he asked harshly. 'Forgive me if I say I doubt that. I doubt that very much.'

Juliet shook her head. 'Surely that's Lady Elinor's business, not yours. It's her ring.'

'It was my mother's,' said Rafe flatly. A bitter smile crossed his dark face. 'The old lady gave it to her on her twenty-first birthday.'

'Oh, God!' Juliet was horrified. 'I had no idea.'

'No.' Rafe believed her.

'She— I— Lady Elinor said she'd been given the ring when she was a girl and I never dreamt—'

'Forget it.' Abruptly Rafe released her, backing off until there was at least an arm's length between them. 'I shouldn't have reacted as I did. The old lady got the ring back when my mother—when she died. I didn't want it and I guess she feels she has the right to do what she likes with it now.'

'But…' Juliet's tongue circled her upper lip. 'I'll give it back,' she said impulsively. 'I don't really need a ring—'

'And have her blame me for ruining her evening? I don't think so.' Rafe was sardonic. 'It's not that important. I shouldn't have mentioned it.'

But it was important and Juliet had the feeling that she knew why Lady Elinor had been so pleased when she'd chosen this particular ring. She'd known Rafe would see it, would recognise it. That was why she'd asked her if he'd seen the ring last night. But Juliet wanted no part of any plan to hurt him.

Shaking her head again, she moved blindly towards the door. She wanted to get out of the studio, out of Polgellin Bay, out of Cary's life and away from Lady Elinor's machinations. The situation was so much more complex than she had ever imagined and she'd had enough.

'I'll see you upstairs,' she said, glancing back at him, and then let out a startled cry when her foot encountered an unexpected obstacle. She'd been so eager to reach the door that led onto the stairs that she hadn't been looking where she was going, and before she knew it she'd stumbled into the canvas he'd placed against the wall when they came in. The canvas teetered, and she grabbed for it, more intent on saving it than herself. And as she did so a handful of sketches fluttered from behind it, spreading themselves decoratively across the floor.

# CHAPTER NINE

AFTERWARDS, she wasn't sure whether it was the sight of the sketches or the fact that she was still unbalanced that had caused her to sway towards the wall. Certainly, the images of Liv Holderness nude body had made her feel slightly faint. Dear God, they were having an affair. Why else would she be reclining on his couch completely naked? No wonder she behaved with such a proprietary air towards him. Didn't he care that she was a married woman?

But then, he hadn't cared that she and Cary were supposed to be engaged either, she reminded herself, a feeling of dizziness making her feel really sick. How dared he criticise Cary? Compared to Rafe...

But her head was swimming and the heat in the room made her feel as if there was no air. She turned bewilderedly, her face mirroring her confusion, and with a muffled oath Rafe lunged across the floor.

'Stupid woman,' he muttered, his arm sliding about her waist, stabilising her with the muscled strength of his body. 'Why the hell didn't you look where you were going? I can just imagine what your fiancé would have thought if you'd reappeared sporting a black eye.'

Juliet was trembling so badly, she could hardly find the words to defend herself. And the truth was, without his support she might still have slid bonelessly to the floor. His heavy breathing revealed the effort he'd made to reach her before she lost consciousness, and it was hard not to feel grateful for his help.

'I should think Cary's opinion is the least of your worries,' she managed at last, trying to steel herself to break away. 'Does Lord Holderness know you're making nude sketches of his wife?'

Rafe sighed. He'd known this was coming, of course, and he cursed himself for leaving the sketches lying about. 'No,' he admitted at last, resisting her feeble efforts to get free of him. Then, deciding he had no choice but to trust her, 'I'm painting her portrait for her husband's birthday. It's supposed to be a surprise, so I'd be grateful if you'd keep it to yourself.'

Juliet caught her breath, and this time she managed to turn and face him. 'You expect me to believe that?' she demanded. 'My God, you must think I came down with the last shower of rain!'

'It's the truth,' said Rafe doggedly, and when she would have turned away he caught her wrist and brought her back to him. 'I don't lie,' he told her harshly. 'If I was having an affair with Liv Holderness, do you think I'd be here alone with you?'

Juliet took a deep breath. 'I asked to see your work,' she said.

'And I was reluctant to show you.'

'Because of Liv.'

'No, because of this,' he muttered thickly and, pulling her into his arms, he lowered his head to hers.

He'd taken advantage of her weakness, she told herself later. That was why she didn't stop him when he parted her lips with his tongue. With the unmistakable pressure of his erection pushing against her stomach, it was far too easy to give in to emotions that had been heightened by their argument. And when she felt his thumbs pushing against the undersides of her breasts, she knew an urgent need to push her hips against his.

Her senses were reeling, and somehow the knowledge that she was supposed to be Cary's fiancée got lost in the sensual pleasure he was arousing in her. The force of her own desire

overcame any latent outrage. She wanted him to kiss her. Dear
God, she wanted him to do so much more than that.

As his mouth ravaged hers, as his tongue pushed deep into
her throat, Rafe felt the wild excitement building inside him take
possession of his reason. He wanted her, he thought. He wanted
her with an urgency he couldn't ever remember feeling before.
They were alone here. Could he really rely on neither Liv nor
Cary interrupting them? He would like to take her on the couch
and wipe the images of Liv's naked body out of her mind.

'I want to make love to you,' he said, his lips finding the moist
curve of her neck, his teeth nipping her flesh with sensual
urgency. Juliet moaned low in her throat and Rafe's hands shook
a little as he peeled her shirt off her shoulders. Her skin was so
soft, the narrow straps of her camisole barely concealing the
tender peaks of her breasts.

He trailed a finger from her jawline, down across her throat
to the dusky hollow just visible above the neckline of the
camisole. Then he bent and followed his finger with his tongue,
licking her and tasting the slightly salty tang of her damp skin.
They were both sweating, he thought. Dammit, his shirt was
sticking to his back. He'd never felt such emotional overload,
never felt the blood thundering so thickly through his veins.

'You taste so good,' he said, and her hands groped blindly for
his face, hot fingers cradling his cheeks, her thumbs moving sensuously against his lips. He couldn't help himself; he opened his
mouth and bit on the soft pad until she whimpered, and then he
tipped the straps of her camisole off her shoulders and buried
his face between her breasts.

Juliet was incapable of resisting. Her body felt hot and alive,
alert to every sensual move he made. With his leg braced
between her thighs, that sensitive part of her was wet and
wanting. His erection pressed against the crotch of her pants,
hard and throbbing with a life of its own.

Rafe was aching with the need to be inside her. All he could
think about was burying himself in her wet heat and letting her

muscles squeeze him until it hurt. He deepened the kiss, backing her up against the wall beside the canvases, bracing himself with his hands on either side of her, pushing his tongue even further into her mouth.

Juliet felt consumed by his hunger. She wound her arms about his neck, pulling him against her, welcoming the carnal rush when his body pinned hers to the wall. She wriggled impatiently, wanting him to touch her everywhere. And particularly that place between her legs that ached for his possession.

'God, keep still!' Rafe muttered hoarsely. He was aware he'd never been so close to losing control in his life. If she didn't stop moving about…

But suddenly, Juliet was stiffening. It was as if the sudden harshness of his words had broken the spell of madness that had gripped them both. 'What did you say?' she demanded unsteadily, her palms now flat against his pectoral muscles, pushing him away, when only moments before she'd been writhing in sexual need.

'Dammit, Juliet—'

'Let me go!'

Rafe gritted his teeth. 'You don't mean that.'

'I do mean it. Let me go!'

'Oh, for God's sake—'

Juliet clenched her teeth. Her shoes weren't stilettos, like Liv's, but he was barefoot, and when she ground her heel into his instep he howled with pain. She felt a moment's remorse as he recoiled and grabbed his foot, hopping on one leg as he sought to restore some feeling to it, but it did give her the opportunity to step away from the wall and straighten her clothes.

'What did you expect?' she asked him bitterly. 'Don't think I don't know what you were trying to do. You thought that by seducing me you could deflect my contempt for the way you're treating Liv's husband. You—you assaulted me. You are totally—totally reprehensible!'

'Oh, grow up!' Rafe was feeling particularly aggrieved at this moment. Apart from the fact that he was suffering the after-effects of her attack, there was a distinct feeling of frustration in his groin. 'My kissing you had nothing to do with those sketches of Liv Holderness. For pity's sake, it's what I do. I'm supposed to be a painter!'

Juliet sniffed. 'All the same—'

'All the same, nothing.' Rafe decided he had nothing to lose by telling the truth. 'You didn't practically cripple me because I kissed you. You just realised you were enjoying yourself and you felt guilty for deceiving Danger Mouse upstairs!'

Rafe was still in a black mood long after Liv had departed.

What he told himself was to his relief Juliet had mentioned nothing of what had passed between them in the studio and she and Cary had left soon afterwards. Liv, however, had been suspicious, but wary, keeping any opinions she might have about their prolonged absence to herself. She knew him well enough to guess that something had happened, but she had more sense than to try and open that particular can of worms today.

Nevertheless, his mood had meant that working was difficult, and with a brief word of apology Rafe had suggested they postpone their appointment until after the weekend was over. 'I've got a headache,' he had said, by way of an excuse, though what he really had was a hard-on that refused to go away.

A cold shower took care of it eventually and he was just stepping out of the cubicle when the phone rang. Grabbing a towel, he wrapped it about his hips, and then strode with some impatience to answer it.

His foot pained him as he paced across the floor and that didn't improve his temper. 'Yes,' he said shortly, hoping it wasn't a client, and then stifled an oath when he heard Lady Elinor's imperious tones.

'Raphael! Raphael, is that you?'

Rafe's jaw tightened. 'As this is my phone in my apartment, I'd say it was a better than average chance that it'd be me,' he responded tersely. 'What do you want, old lady? I thought you'd be too busy to talk to me today.'

There was a long silence and Rafe wondered if he'd been too curt with her. Dammit, it wasn't her fault that he was in danger of screwing up his life. He didn't know what it was about Juliet, but she pushed all the wrong buttons. Or were they all the right ones? Either way, it would be safer if he didn't see her again.

'You sound as if you've been ridden hard and put away wet,' said Lady Elinor eventually, and he realised, that whatever it was she wanted, she was prepared to humour him to get it. 'Have you seen Cary?'

Rafe expelled a sharp breath, the images her words had evoked causing an unwelcome tightness in his gut. 'Why would you ask that?' he queried, wondering if Juliet had said something, after all. But no. She and Cary had hardly had time to get back to Tregellin, always assuming that was where they had been heading.

'Because I believe he and Juliet were going into Polgellin Bay this morning,' Lady Elinor replied smoothly. 'I know Juliet wanted to see your work.'

'They've been and gone,' said Rafe shortly, deciding there was no point in prevaricating. If he didn't tell her, Cary surely would. The fact that Liv had been here, too, would ensure a discreet—or in Cary's case not so discreet—disclosure.

'And did you show her some of your paintings?' the old lady persisted. 'She's such a nice girl, isn't she? Not at all what we expected.'

'You mean, what *you* expected,' Rafe corrected her grimly. 'I didn't have an opinion either way.'

'But you've met her now,' Lady Elinor pointed out. 'You must have formed some opinion as to her character. Josie tells me the pair of you spent some time talking together last evening.'

Rafe's teeth ground together. 'What do you want me to say, old lady? That I like her? That I envy Cary his good fortune? You like her. Isn't that enough for you?'

'Raphael, Raphael, I'm only asking for your opinion.'

'Really?' Rafe felt driven. Then he said the unforgivable, 'Do you think I want to have sex with her? Is that what you want to hear?'

If he'd expected the old lady to be offended he was disappointed. The peal of laughter that she uttered came clearly over the phone. 'And do you?' she asked, causing him no small measure of frustration. 'Poor Cary. He has no idea what he's up against.'

Rafe's free hand balled into a fist. 'You can be a nasty old woman sometimes,' he said, not caring at that moment what she thought of him. 'Look, is this going somewhere? Because I have to tell you, I'm standing here with just a towel to cover me.'

There was another silence and then Lady Elinor said, 'So you're not going to talk about her?'

'What's to say? You evidently like her.' He scowled. 'Enough to give her my mother's ring.'

'Ah!' Rafe had the feeling that that was what the old lady had been waiting for. 'You noticed.'

Rafe closed his eyes for a moment. 'I couldn't help but notice, could I?'

'If you say so, my dear. Do I take it you object to my generosity? Or is it that you're afraid Cary might pawn the ring before you can get it back?'

Rafe heaved a sigh and opened his eyes again. 'There's no chance of that, is there?' He felt weary suddenly. 'In any case, it was your ring to begin with. You can do what you like with it.'

'Yes, I suppose I can.' Lady Elinor sounded thoughtful for a moment. 'But, in any case, that's not why I rang you. I want you to come to dinner this evening. You've not got a previous engagement, have you?'

Rafe's jaw dropped. 'You're joking!'

'No.' The old lady was annoyingly smug. 'I was going to ask old Charteris to join us, but on second thoughts, I prefer to ask you.'

'No way.'

'Raphael, don't be like that. You wouldn't want your grand-mother to be the odd one out, would you?' She paused. 'The Holdernesses are coming, you know.'

'And that would interest me because…?'

'I understood that you and Lady Holderness were old friends.'

'We are friends. Or, at least, we've known one another for a number of years.' He sighed. 'I've told you what the situation is with Liv. She was here this morning, actually. She and your guests arrived together.'

'How cosy!' Lady Elinor was sardonic. 'Well? What do you say?'

'About tonight?'

'What else?'

Rafe's stomach clenched. He knew that going to Tregellin again while Juliet was there was not a good idea. God, hadn't he just been telling himself that? And seeing her with Cary… His shoulders hunched defensively. He would be all kinds of an idiot if he agreed to the old lady's request…

Juliet prepared for the dinner party without enthusiasm. But, she reminded herself, this was their last evening at Tregellin. In the morning they'd be leaving, and she could put all thoughts of Rafe Marchese out of her head.

And she could forget about what had happened that morning, she added tersely. For heaven's sake, what had she been thinking of, allowing that man to touch her again? Particularly after what she'd just learned about him. The man was totally unscrupulous; totally without shame.

As for that story about him painting Liv Holderness portrait: well, was it likely that Lord Holderness—whoever he was—would want everyone to see a portrait of his wife in the nude? Of course, it was just the sort of idea Liv might have had, to give her an excuse to visit Rafe's studio. But however good the sketches had been, there was no way they were going to be enlarged into a full portrait.

Full-blown portrait, perhaps, she thought maliciously. Yet despite her reservations, she had to admit Rafe's talent was an awesome thing. Just a glimpse of those sketches, and she'd known at once who his subject had been. Which wasn't always easy with a nude.

She sighed, trying not to think about the morning. What she should be worrying about was what might happen if he chose to tell his grandmother her tawdry little secret. Cary would be hopelessly humiliated. He'd never forgive her for making him look a fool.

Yet, would that be such a bad thing? she asked herself. Even before this morning, she'd been feeling bad about deceiving Lady Elinor in this way. If she had half the old lady's character, she'd walk out right now. The trouble was, she didn't have the train fare back to London.

No, she would have to stay until tomorrow. And she supposed she owed it to herself to carry the evening off in a way that would have made her father proud of her. If he could see what she was doing, she hoped he'd forgive her. She wasn't a bad person, she told herself. Just pathetically naïve and weak.

The black dress with its satin lining and chiffon sleeves was attractive. A lace overdress ended some inches above her knees, but sheer black stockings hid her slender thighs from view. Four-inch heels threatened a twisted ankle, but they were the only shoes that matched the rest of her outfit.

She hesitated over what earrings to wear and finally settled on gold loops that complemented her necklace. A handful of narrow bracelets circled one wrist while the watch her father had given her for her eighteenth birthday circled the other. She slipped the ruby onto her finger with some reluctance. Since Rafe had told her whose ring it really was she felt even worse about wearing it.

Still, Rafe wouldn't be present this evening so she could relax. And she might even make a point of forgetting the ring tomorrow morning and face Cary's displeasure once they were safely back in London. He could hardly penalise her then, when she'd done everything he'd asked of her. If he guessed she'd left the ring behind deliberately, so be it. It wasn't his ring and she was unlikely to see him again once this weekend was over.

With one final critical glance at her appearance, Juliet tucked a strand of hair behind her ear and left the room. It was still early. Barely half-past seven, in fact, but she suspected Lady Elinor would be waiting in the drawing room, ready to greet her guests. The Holdernesses might already have arrived. From the little she knew of Lady Holderness, she knew she wasn't the retiring type!

She heard voices as she crossed the hall and her nerves tightened. She'd already lied to four people and she wasn't looking forward to lying to a fifth. What if someone asked a question she couldn't answer? Cary was no help. He'd been pathetically eager to abandon her the night before.

She was so tense that for a moment, when she reached the doorway, she thought she must be hallucinating. The man who was standing on the hearth, one arm resting on the mantel, one foot raised to support itself on the brass fender, was so familiar to her. All in black this evening—black pleated trousers, black turtle-neck and a black velvet jacket—Rafe looked completely at ease in these surroundings. The sweat-stained individual who'd greeted them that morning, or the barefoot artist in jeans and T-shirt with whom she'd shared those devastating kisses, might have been from another planet. This was Rafe Marchese, Lady Elinor's grandson, and anyone who thought differently should definitely think again.

Juliet swallowed and Lady Elinor, who was once again seated on the sofa, raised a welcoming hand. 'Come in, my dear,' she said as Rafe straightened away from the mantel. 'I thought I'd ask Raphael to join us. Raphael, why don't you ask Juliet what she'd like to drink?'

# CHAPTER TEN

THE Holdernesses evidently hadn't yet arrived and it was obvious that Lady Elinor expected Juliet to accompany Rafe to the drinks cabinet and tell him what she'd like. In truth, a stiff vodka wouldn't have come amiss but, in the circumstances, she might be wise to keep her wits about her.

'What'll it be?' asked Rafe, aware of her reluctance to be anywhere near him and disliking the connotations. Dammit, he didn't want to be here either. But it had been even harder finding an excuse and the last thing he wanted to do was give the old lady any reason to suspect what had been going on. 'Sherry— or just plain old hemlock over ice?'

Juliet cast a resentful glance in his direction. 'I suppose you're enjoying this, aren't you?' she whispered accusingly. 'Why didn't you tell me you were coming here tonight?'

'Me?' Rafe arched a mocking eyebrow.

'Us,' Juliet corrected hastily. 'I meant us.'

Rafe shrugged. 'Would you believe I didn't know myself until later in the day?'

'No.'

'Nevertheless, it's true.' Rafe told himself he didn't care if she believed him or not. 'The old lady likes to keep her guests on their toes. Haven't you realised that yet?'

Juliet moistened her dry lips. 'I haven't been here long

enough to make any assessment of her character,' she replied stiffly, and Rafe gave a reluctant smile.

'Haven't you?' He shook his head. 'I feel as if you've been here for weeks.'

Juliet regarded him defensively. 'Why do I get the feeling that's not a compliment?' She dragged her eyes away from him, trying to concentrate on why she was here. But it was difficult when standing so close to him reminded her so vividly of the heat of his body, the faintly citrus scent that mingled with the clean smell of man.

But then she remembered the sketches…

'What are you two doing?' Rafe wasn't surprised at the old lady's irritation. 'Don't you know it's rude to whisper?'

Juliet swung round. 'I'm sorry—'

'She hasn't decided what she wants yet,' said Rafe obliquely. 'Come on, Juliet. Make up your mind.'

Juliet cast him a venomous look. 'Sherry,' she said abruptly. 'I'll have sherry.' And, reluctantly, 'Thank you.'

'My pleasure.' Rafe sought his own relief in mockery, grateful when Juliet went to sit beside their hostess.

Lady Elinor regarded Juliet closely. 'What has Raphael been saying to you? Is something wrong?'

Juliet felt the colour flooding her throat. 'No,' she denied unconvincingly. 'I— Rafe—I mean, Raphael was just offering suggestions about—about what I should drink.'

'Is that all?' Lady Elinor looked up as her grandson came over to hand Juliet her glass of sherry. 'You haven't been intimidating this young woman, have you, Raphael?'

Rafe straightened. 'Now, why would you think a thing like that, old lady?' He glanced at Juliet's bent head. 'We hardly know one another.'

'But she did visit your studio this morning,' Lady Elinor persisted as Juliet's fingers tightened around the glass. She turned once again to her female guest. 'Did Raphael show you some of his work?'

Juliet couldn't escape an answer. 'Oh, yes,' she said, making sure she didn't look in Rafe's direction, but the old lady clicked her tongue with some impatience.

'And?' she prompted. 'What did you think? Has the boy got any talent?'

*The boy!* Juliet suppressed a groan. 'I'm—sure he has,' she murmured uncomfortably. 'But—I'm no expert.' She glanced up at Rafe, wondering what he'd do if she told his grandmother what she'd seen. She didn't think she wanted to find out.

'The stock answer,' said Lady Elinor irritably. 'You live in London, don't you? You must have visited other galleries.'

'I don't have a gallery, old lady,' Rafe intervened, aware of Juliet's ambivalence. 'And you can't expect Juliet to give you a report when you won't even come and see for yourself.'

'Of course, you would say that,' retorted Lady Elinor tersely. 'Oh, where's Cary? He must know that the Holdernesses will be here soon.'

'Actually, I thought one of the paintings he showed me was amazingly good,' Juliet burst out suddenly, surprising herself, and then wished she hadn't been so impulsive when her supposed fiancé sauntered into the room.

'Really?' Despite the fact that moments before she'd been deploring her other grandson's tardiness, now Lady Elinor ignored him to stare at Juliet with sharp, assessing eyes. 'So why didn't you say this when I asked you? Why did you let me think that you hadn't been impressed with Raphael's work?'

'Because she wasn't!' exclaimed Cary scornfully, immediately latching on to the conversation. 'My God, Grandmama, is that why you sent us there? To act as your unpaid spies?'

'Unpaid?' His grandmother regarded him without liking. 'Be careful what you say, Cary. For someone who makes his living hustling at a casino, I don't think you should criticise your cousin for trying to make a success of his life.'

Cary's jaw dropped in consternation and Juliet saw Rafe turn away from the younger man's embarrassment. 'Who told you I worked in a casino?' Cary demanded, his eyes moving suspiciously from Juliet to Rafe and back again. 'If Jules has—'

'It wasn't your fiancée,' replied Lady Elinor contemptuously. 'Or Raphael, before your suspicions turn in that direction. I'm not a complete fool, Cary. I have friends in the City. They keep me informed of what you're doing. And why not? You have nothing to hide, do you?'

'No!'

Cary was indignant, but his reddening face gave the lie to his words, and once again Juliet wished she'd never allowed herself to get involved in his affairs. No matter what she thought of Rafe's behaviour, her own was so much worse.

Relief came with the sound of a car outside and then voices in the hall heralded the arrival of Lady Elinor's other guests. The old lady got to her feet herself to greet Lord and Lady Holderness and, if she considered Liv's slashed neckline and silky harem pants hardly suitable for an informal dinner party, no one would have guessed from her benign expression.

Robert Holderness was a man in his late fifties, whose genial demeanour disguised an evident pride in his young wife. Wearing a dark dinner jacket and tie, he ushered Liv into the room ahead of him, nodding a greeting to Rafe before going to take Lady Elinor's outstretched hand.

'Sorry we're late, Ellie,' he said, and for a moment Juliet didn't know who he was talking to. Then Elinor—*Ellie*—clicked into place, and as she showed her comprehension she saw Rafe watching her from across the room.

'Think nothing of it, Bob,' Lady Elinor assured him pleasantly. 'And this must be your new wife. Olivia, isn't it? Raphael tells me that you and he are old friends.'

Liv looked slightly taken aback for once. 'I— Yes,' she said, clearly not expecting to be welcomed in such a manner. She licked her lips nervously. 'What a—lovely home you have, Lady Elinor.'

'I like it.' The old lady's answer made no allowance for the fact that the place was practically falling about her ears. Rafe thought that only someone of Lady Elinor's breeding could say a thing like that and get away with it. She gestured towards the tray of drinks. 'Raphael, perhaps you'd offer our guests an aperitif?'

'I'll do it.' Cary brushed rudely past his cousin and positioned himself beside the cabinet. 'What'll you have, my lord? Scotch and soda? A Martini?'

'Perhaps you should ask my wife first,' Lord Holderness declared a little testily. He turned to Liv. 'What would you like, my dear?'

'Oh—um, a little white wine, please,' she said, though Juliet noticed her eyes were on Rafe, not Cary. 'I think you should have the same, darling. You know what Dr Charteris said.'

'Charteris is an old woman,' declared her husband shortly, and Lady Elinor, who had resumed her seat, clapped her hands.

'Bravo,' she said. 'I totally agree with you, Bob. But,' her eyes turned towards Juliet, 'I haven't introduced you to my other guest. You haven't met Cary's fiancée, Juliet, have you?'

'Why, no.' Lord Holderness came to shake Juliet's hand warmly. 'How do you do, my dear?' He glanced at the younger man. 'I didn't even know your grandson had a regular girlfriend.'

'Nor did we,' murmured Lady Elinor drily, but her smile for Juliet begged forgiveness.

'Let me introduce you to my wife,' Lord Holderness continued, still speaking to Juliet. 'I'm sure you and she will have much more in common. What do you say, Olivia?'

Juliet thought Liv looked a little sick now, but she couldn't find it in her heart to feel sympathy for her. For heaven's sake, the woman was cheating on her husband. How defensible was that?

'As a matter of fact—' she began, ignoring the plea in the other woman's eyes, but before she could reveal that she'd met Lady Holderness earlier in the day Cary interrupted them.

'That's two white wines, then, is it?' he asked, clearly resenting the fact that he was being sidelined, and Liv turned grate-fully in his direction.

'Please,' she said. 'If that's all right with you, Bobby?'

'Whatever Lady Holderness says,' her husband declared, making it obvious that he expected Cary to treat his wife with respect. 'I just do as I'm told.'

'Oh, Bobby, that's not true,' Liv protested, once again jumping in before Juliet could speak, and Lady Elinor took the opportunity to invite her to sit beside her on the sofa.

'I want to hear all about how you two met,' she said firmly. 'Bob is so shy when it comes to personal details.'

Liv looked decidedly nervous now and Juliet couldn't blame her on that score. She'd experienced a similar interrogation the first evening she was here and Liv had so much more to hide than most.

'So—Juliet, is it?—how long have you and Ellie's grandson been seeing one another?' Juliet was distracted by Lord Holderness who had evidently decided to conduct his own in-vestigation. 'Did you meet before he went to South Africa?'

'I—well, yes, we did,' Juliet was fumbling, when to her com-plete surprise Rafe came to her rescue.

'They met when they were children,' he said, strolling over to join them. 'Isn't that right, Cary? Before you came to live here, wasn't it?'

Cary handed out the glasses of wine he was carrying and then gave his cousin a resentful look. 'You know it was,' he said, without gratitude, and Rafe's lips tilted in amusement.

'I thought so,' he said drily, making Juliet wonder what else he knew as well.

But, watching them, she felt powerless to intervene. She might believe Rafe was only using Cary to protect his own re-lationship with Liv Holderness, but now that the moment had gone, she baulked at telling the old man his wife was having an affair with a younger man. Lord Holderness seemed too genuine an individual to hurt like that.

Thankfully, Cary seemed more intent on improving the impression Lord Holderness had of him than arguing with Rafe and, slipping a possessive arm about Juliet's waist, he said, 'I consider myself a very lucky man, my lord.'

Rafe, viewing Cary's actions with unjustified irritation, clenched his teeth. Just watching his cousin lay his hands on Juliet aroused a gnawing hunger inside him that wouldn't go away. He badly wanted to tear Cary away from her; to draw her out of there—by her hair, if necessary—and show her she was wasting her time on such a sorry piece of dirt.

Which was so unlike him, he thought, trying to concentrate on the conversation. Keeping his eyes away from Juliet's slightly flushed face, he tried to rationalise what was happening to him. God, he was no caveman, desperate to show how macho he was. But for the first time in his life, he had to accept that Juliet aroused feelings inside him that refused to be rationalised. He wanted her, he acknowledged frustratedly. Or perhaps, less emotively, he wanted to sleep with her. Maybe then he'd be able to get on with his life.

Tuning back into the conversation, he heard Cary saying, 'I'm sure you consider yourself a very lucky man, too,' and Lord Holderness gave a grunt of agreement.

'I do indeed,' he said, taking a sip of his wine. 'Thank you.'

'Yes, Liv's a damn fine woman,' Cary continued, obviously not appreciating that he was treading on dangerous ground. 'I've always thought so.'

As Rafe had anticipated, the old man's eyes narrowed suspiciously. 'You know my wife, Daniels?'

'Oh…' Cary reddened. 'Well, yeah. Everybody knows her!' he exclaimed uncomfortably. And then, compounding his error, 'Only by reputation, of course.'

'By reputation!'

Lord Holderness was fairly breathing fire now and once again Rafe felt compelled to intervene. 'I think what Cary means is that as she's Ken Melrose's daughter, she's naturally met a lot of people,' he said mildly. 'Isn't that right, Cary?'

'Well, yeah,' muttered Cary again, though the look he cast in his cousin's direction was hardly grateful.

'I assume you mean because her father owns the Dragon Hotel,' Lord Holderness said, somewhat mollified. 'But she never worked in the bar, you know.'

Didn't she? Rafe exchanged a speaking glance with the woman in question, but he didn't contradict the old man. Josie's appearance to announce that dinner was waiting was a welcome relief to all of them.

They were eating in the conservatory instead of the somewhat questionable dignity of the formal dining room, but Lady Elinor presided over the table with all the elegance of her ancestors. The fact that on his arrival that evening Rafe had had to help Josie carry the small table out of the morning room and set it up in its present position wasn't mentioned, or that it was he who'd suggested to the housekeeper that a cold starter might be in order, thus saving the old woman from bustling back and forth with hot plates on two occasions.

The seating arrangements were of Lady Elinor's choosing. Significantly, she'd seated herself and Lord Holderness at opposite ends of the table, with Juliet and Cary on one side and Olivia and Rafe on the other. It meant that Juliet was conscious of Rafe's eyes upon her with disturbing frequency throughout the meal, which wasn't tempered by Cary's indignation that his grandmother had placed Rafe opposite him, thus acknowledging his cousin's right to be there.

'What the hell does she think she's doing?' he muttered to Juliet as the other members of the party were debating the pros and cons of Cornwall's bid for independence. 'This is to punish me, isn't it? Because she's discovered that I'm not working at some prissy job in the City.'

'He is your cousin,' pointed out Juliet in an undertone, having no desire to defend Rafe, but aware of the dangers here. 'For goodness' sake, Cary, what does it matter? We're going home tomorrow.'

'I know.' Cary's jaw set belligerently. 'But you have to wonder what he says to her when I'm not here.'

'You're getting paranoid,' protested Juliet impatiently, and then flushed when she found Rafe's eyes on her again. Goodness, she fretted, was reading lips another of his accomplishments? She wouldn't be at all surprised. Lifting her table napkin to her lips, she used it to screen her next words. 'Don't forget, he got you out of a sticky situation earlier on.'

'Yeah. I wonder why.' Cary was unappeased. 'What do you think? Are he and Liv having an affair? She seemed bloody familiar with his apartment, if you ask me. And she didn't like it when you and he went down to his studio on your own, however amenable she might have appeared.'

Juliet's stomach tightened unpleasantly. Hearing her own opinion voiced by another person was so much worse than believing she was the only one who knew the truth. And for all she told herself she hated the way Rafe had behaved towards her, the memory of how she'd felt when he was kissing her was a constant torment.

'You're not eating, Juliet.'

Lady Elinor had noticed that, although she'd taken a few mouthfuls of the chilled consommé that had started the meal, so far she'd barely touched the rosemary-flavoured chicken, whose crisp skin made her feel slightly sick.

'Oh—I'm not very hungry,' she murmured awkwardly.

'You don't like chicken, perhaps?'

'Heavens, yes.' Juliet was conscious of everyone looking at her now. 'It's not the food—'

'Then, what—?'

'You're embarrassing her, old lady.' Rafe regarded his grandmother over the rim of his glass. 'She's not as used to you as we are. Why don't you turn your considerable energies towards ringing the bell for Josie? I'm sure your other guests would like another bottle of this excellent Chardonnay.'

Lady Elinor's lips pursed. 'I'll thank you to keep your opinions to yourself, Raphael,' she declared irritably, and Juliet was aware of Cary's chortle of triumph at what he saw as Rafe's humiliation.

But Rafe's words did have the desired effect and a moment later Lady Elinor reached for the bellpull and gave it a sharp jerk. However, Rafe noticed that it didn't stop her from casting a speculative glance from him to Juliet and back again, and he knew his defence of the girl hadn't gone unnoticed. He just hoped he hadn't overplayed his hand.

After dessert—a delicious summer pudding that Juliet suspected might have been bought in for the occasion—they all retired to the drawing room again for coffee. This time Cary made sure he was seated near Lord Holderness, and when Josie had delivered the tray and departed he started the conversation by saying, ingenuously, 'Grandmama tells me you live in a castle, sir. How exciting! Is it very old?'

Lord Holderness frowned. 'What have you been saying, Ellie?' he asked half-impatiently. 'You know perfectly well that Trelawney is just a country house.'

Lady Elinor's lips tightened. 'I believe what I actually said was that Trelawney looked a little like a castle,' she declared, giving her younger grandson an impatient look. 'Besides, I can't see that it's of any interest to you, Cary.'

'Oh, you're wrong. I'm always interested in old buildings,' he protested with assumed innocence. 'I mean, I'm always amazed at how much it costs for the upkeep these days. I can't imagine how you—all—manage it.'

Juliet was horrified now. She thought she knew exactly where this was going, and she tried to catch Cary's eye to warn him not to say any more. But her 'fiancé' was enjoying himself for the first time that evening, unaware that he might just alienate himself from the one person who cared anything about him.

'Nevertheless, we do,' Lord Holderness responded stiffly. 'It would be a terrible shame if one's heritage had to be sacrificed on the altar of commercialism.'

'I agree.' Cary was endeavouring to sound sincere. 'I know I love this old place, but you must have noticed how it's deteriorating. I wish there was a way I could help you, Grandmama.' He frowned as if he'd just thought of it. 'Have you ever thought of selling some of the land that's at present part of the estate? To give you some working capital, so to speak.'

'That will do, Cary.'

It was Rafe who spoke. He'd been lounging on the sofa beside Lady Elinor, jacket parted, long legs extended and crossed at the ankles. But now he sat up, and Juliet could see he was furious. She was fairly annoyed herself, she thought, and she wasn't even a member of the family. Didn't Cary realise he was in danger of betraying the fact that he'd read that letter from the developer?

'I don't believe I spoke to you,' Cary said now, scowling at Rafe for involving himself in the discussion. He turned to the old lady again. 'You must agree with me, Grandmama. Tregellin is going to collapse about your ears unless something is done.'

'Cary—'

'It's all right, Raphael.' Lady Elinor placed a hand upon his knee, indicating that she didn't need his assistance. 'Cary has his own opinions, of course. And I'm interested in how he feels about Tregellin. I must take his suggestion of selling the property seriously.'

'Not the house,' broke in Cary at once, apparently realising his mistake. 'Just—one or two of the farms, perhaps.' He cast about him for someone to support his argument. 'Jules, you can see the sense in what I'm saying, can't you? No one wants to see the old place fall apart.'

Before Juliet could say anything, Lady Elinor spoke. 'I believe I know what's best for Tregellin, Cary,' she murmured, and, judging from her expression, Juliet didn't think Cary understood his grandmother at all. 'Now,' she turned to Lord Holderness, 'does your wife play bridge, Bob?'

She didn't, but her hostess prevailed upon her to learn and, together with Cary, who was eager to mend fences, they made a four. 'You don't mind, do you, Juliet?' the old lady asked, before they gathered round the table in the conservatory again. 'Raphael, you'll entertain our young guest, won't you? You might show her your mother's paintings. You'll find one or two in the library.'

# CHAPTER ELEVEN

RAFE pushed open the library door and allowed a reluctant Juliet to precede him into the room. He was trying hard to hide his frustration at the way Lady Elinor had manipulated him, aware that he was the last person Juliet wanted to spend any more time with.

Not that he'd wanted to join the bridge party. Far from it. But he resented the old lady's machinations almost as much as Cary did. Dammit, he didn't want to spend the rest of the evening with a woman who didn't trust him. Not when being with her was both a betrayal of his own self-respect and an intolerable temptation.

Another source of irritation was the apparent presence of some of his mother's paintings. In all the time he'd lived at Tregellin, he never remembered seeing any of her water colours on public view. In fact, he'd always assumed that the old lady had destroyed any that had come into her possession after his mother's death.

Now, however, when he followed Juliet into the library, which had also acted as his grandfather's study when he was alive, he caught his breath in stunned disbelief. Two walls were, as usual, lined with the books that had been collected over the years, but the others were a veritable art gallery of not just his mother's paintings, but also his own.

Pastel impressions of the shifting light on the canals of Venice mingled with Cornish landscapes that were harsh and rugged, and scarred with old mine-workings; vanilla skies above purple Tuscan hills were offset by a rocky coastline that despite its silvery sands was intrinsically English. Some of his own work, paintings he'd assumed had been sold to anonymous collectors, were his earliest efforts, landscapes that these days wouldn't survive his personal cutting floor.

'*Dios,*' he said succinctly, backing up against the door to close it, leaning against the panels for a moment, too dazed to move.

Juliet turned to give him a resentful look. 'Hey, I don't like this any more than you do!' she exclaimed. And then, noticing his stunned expression, 'What's wrong?'

Rafe grunted. 'Nothing. Everything.' He stared at the paintings. 'I wonder how long the old lady has had these?'

'Your mother's paintings?' Juliet moved closer to the wall. 'I assume these water colours are hers?'

Rafe nodded. 'She loved Italy. Particularly Tuscany.' Then, as if trying to clear his head. 'We spent a lot of time there when I was young.'

Juliet gave him a curious look. 'How old were you when your mother died?' she ventured, and then shook her head. 'Don't answer that. It's nothing to do with me.'

Rafe answered her anyway. 'I was seven,' he said flatly. He bent his head, 'There was no one to look after me, so the authorities sent me to England.'

'To your grandmother?'

'To the old lady, yes,' agreed Rafe, pressing his shoulders back against the door behind him. 'I hated it at first. England was so cold!'

Juliet thought she could imagine how terrifying it must have been for him, a small boy, uprooted from everything he knew and was used to, from his paternal heritage, in fact. She wanted to ask where his father had been at that time, but that would be too intrusive. All the same, she had to know why the pictures had come as such a surprise to him.

Glancing over her shoulder, she said, 'And you didn't know

Lady Elinor had these paintings?' she asked tentatively. 'But if they were here—'

'They weren't.' Rafe raked agitated fingers over his skull. 'I was here, in this room, less than a week ago.' His lips twisted. 'They weren't here then and nor were the others.'

'Your paintings, you mean?'

'If you can call them that.' Rafe was bitter. 'I painted these— oh, maybe fifteen years ago.'

'And what happened to them?'

'I got a call from a solicitor in Bodmin, who said he'd heard about my work through his connections with the school where I was teaching. He came to see them, said he liked them. I considered myself lucky to have found a buyer.' He gave a short, mirthless laugh. 'I even pitied the poor devil for taking them on.'

Juliet stared at him. 'Don't be so critical. I think they're very good. This solicitor must have thought so, anyway.'

'Oh, no.' Rafe pushed away from the door and strode across the room fairly radiating controlled violence. 'Don't you see— there was no solicitor? It was the old lady manipulating me again.' He paused. 'I was still living here, at Tregellin. I didn't have a place of my own, but she knew I'd converted one of the old coach houses into a makeshift studio, and she lost no opportunity to ridicule my efforts, to tell me that I'd never succeed in producing anything worthwhile. She used to tell my mother the same thing. That's why Christina—that was my mother's name—refused to come back to England. The old lady wanted to control her life, just as she'd like to control mine.'

Juliet frowned. 'So why do you think she bought the paintings?'

'Who knows? Another of her games, perhaps. If, by some incredible chance, I became successful, she could produce these and claim she'd always known I had talent.' He snorted. 'If not, no one would be any the wiser.'

Juliet shook her head. 'Do you really believe she's that devious?'

Rafe scowled. 'She can be,' he said, 'so beware.'

Juliet caught her breath. Was he warning her that Lady Elinor might have an agenda for her, too? She'd certainly thwarted Cary's attempt to outwit her. About his job, at least.

'It's nothing to do with me,' she said again, not wanting to take sides, but to her dismay Rafe came to stand directly in front of her.

'It will be when you marry Cary,' he said, lifting a hand and smearing his thumb across her lower lip. It was an incredibly sensuous thing to do and she wondered if his anger had blinded him to his actions. His eyes darkened. 'Are you really going to marry that sorry excuse for a man?'

'He's not a sorry excuse for a man.' Juliet was defensive. 'And you're hardly in a position to judge.' She jerked her head to one side to avoid his intimate caress, but all she did was shift his focus, long fingers curving about the taut muscles at the back of her neck.

She was intensely conscious of him, of the fluid strength with which he held her as he probed the sensitive nerves that bracketed her spine. Her mouth dried, her protests shrivelling in spite of her resistance. All she was really conscious of were his eyes upon her, watching her closely, like a predator preparing to strike.

'Go on,' he taunted at last. 'Say what you have to. You despise me. I can see that. But what is there about Cary that rings your bell? Tell me about him. Tell me how much you love him. What does he have that attracts you? Is it his personality? His good looks? What?'

'I don't have to tell you anything,' retorted Juliet, and Rafe was infuriated by the fact that, once again, she was making him act like a savage. But damn it all, he thought, seeing those paintings had brought out the worst in him. As the old lady had known they would, he guessed bitterly. But even she couldn't have had this scenario in mind.

'Cat got your tongue?' he mocked now, ignoring the insistent voice inside him that kept warning him to end this, while he still could. 'For someone who professes to be engaged to someone else, you're very permissive. Tell me, were you thinking about Cary when I was kissing you, when I was pushing my tongue into your mouth—?'

'Stop it!'

Juliet brought up her hands to push against his chest, but when her fingers spread against the fine fabric of his sweater all she was conscious of was the body beneath the cloth. She could feel his heart beating, a living, breathing force that seemed to surround her, and a trickle of moisture made its way down between her breasts.

'What's he like in bed?' Rafe was relentless, the demon on his shoulder finding pleasure in her weak efforts to escape him. He defended his actions by assuring himself that his grandmother shouldn't have provoked him, but he couldn't help wondering if he was just playing into her hands. 'Is he better or worse than your ex-husband?' he jeered softly. 'I guess he must be *much* better. Why else would you be marrying the poor sod?'

'You have no right to criticise Cary,' Juliet protested unsteadily. 'At least he's not having an affair with a married woman!'

'I'm not having an affair with a married woman!' Rafe shifted to catch her chin in a brutal grip, his fingers digging into her soft flesh. He stared down at her with narrowed eyes. 'If those sketches are still bugging you, I explained what I was doing. Why is it so hard to believe that Liv would come to me?'

'Oh, I have no difficulty in believing that Liv comes to you,' retorted Juliet contemptuously. 'Where else would she go when she wants a younger man in her bed?'

'You're crazy!' Rafe was incensed. 'Liv loves her husband. Just because you got your knickers in a twist when you saw she was naked in those sketches, don't imagine I feel the same.'

'They don't turn you on, then?'

'Hell, no!'

'Oh, please—'

'I mean it.' Rafe swore. 'If I'd been turned on by every nude I'd seen, I'd be in a constant state of arousal.'

'You're disgusting!'

'And you're incredible,' said Rafe harshly. 'If I didn't know better I'd say Cary had dreamed the whole thing up to protect his own sorry ass.' His lips twisted. 'And you're no better. You're prepared to prostitute yourself to get a share of the old lady's cash—'

His words were arrested by the simple fact of Juliet's palm hitting his cheek. She'd pulled her hands free and her fingers stung from their violent contact with his face.

'You—you—' she choked, unable to find an epithet to suit the occasion, and saw the bitter smile that crossed his face.

'Hey, call me a bastard, why don't you?' he taunted. 'You wouldn't be the first.' He pushed her away from him so violently that she almost fell. 'You're just like the old lady, do you know that? You don't like to hear the truth, even when it jumps up and hits you in the face!'

'It's not true!'

Juliet swallowed convulsively, aware that the little she'd eaten at dinner was in danger of making a return appearance. She'd known he had the ability to hurt her, but not how much, and with a muffled moan she turned and headed for the door.

He didn't try to stop her, and upstairs, in her room, she made straight for the lavatory. Her stomach heaved on cue and, after a few exhausting minutes, she transferred to the hand basin.

She was struggling to clean her teeth, to get the unpleasant taste out of her mouth, when there was a knock at the outer door. She stiffened instinctively, but then, realising Rafe was unlikely to come after her, let alone know which room she was occupying, she wiped her mouth with the back of her hand and walked across the sitting room to the door.

'Who is it?' she called, but no one answered. Neither was the knock repeated, and, rueing the fact that the door didn't have a peephole as hotel doors did, she reluctantly cracked it open.

Rafe was standing outside, his hands hanging loosely at his sides, a look of weary resignation on his dark face. She would have slammed the door again, but he put his foot in the opening, pressing it wider with one hand and easing his way inside.

'I'm sorry,' he said simply, her white face and bruised eyes telling it all. Reaching out, he grabbed her hips and pulled her towards him. 'I'm such a fool,' he said, burying his face in the hollow of her neck. 'Please: tell me you forgive me.'

Juliet couldn't speak. She was trembling so badly that she was amazed her legs continued to support her. She needed to sit down, she thought. *Or lie down*, another less virtuous voice insinuated. Which made her no better than Liv.

'Oh, sweetheart.' One hand cupped her nape and her eyes closed as his mouth descended towards hers. Firm lips rubbed gently against hers, his tongue a tender caress now as he parted her mouth and pushed inside. Sensuously, sensually, he coaxed her tongue into a helpless participation and then, as his own needs sharpened, he deepened the kiss until any will she might have had to resist him was totally destroyed.

His kisses drugged her senses, bruised her lips, robbed her of the breath in her lungs. He had a hand at her back, sliding possessively over her bottom, urging her even closer against him until his erection pressed against her mound.

'You knew I'd come to find you, didn't you?' he challenged when his mouth seared her cheek. His tongue found the erratic pulse that beat beneath her ear and which matched his own. He was struggling to hang on to his senses, but with her in his arms it was hard to keep his head.

'N—no. No.' Her response was husky, her voice losing definition as his fingers slid down to her thigh to lift her leg and wind it about his hip. 'I—I didn't even know you knew which room I was sleeping in.'

'Oh, I knew,' muttered Rafe, his hand slipping beneath the short hem of her dress to caress her. 'The old lady told me. But I doubt if even she had anything like this in mind.'

Juliet sucked in a breath as his long fingers moved over the fine silk of her stockings and found smooth bare skin. Between her legs she knew she was wet and vulnerable, and his muffled groan of satisfaction proved he had discovered that, too.

'You want me,' he said, and his words were shaken, as if, in spite of everything, he hadn't been entirely sure of himself, after all.

'Don't talk,' she said, cupping his face in her hands, feeling his stubble against her palms. She brought his lips back to hers. 'This is a much more satisfying use of your mouth.'

'I can think of a better one,' said Rafe harshly, but she noticed he didn't refuse her invitation. Angling her face to his, he captured her lower lip between his teeth, biting the soft flesh with a fierceness that was as sexual as it was painful.

Juliet clung, fisting handfuls of his silk sweater, uncaring that she was pulling his chest hair out by its roots. Only when he stifled a gasp did she realise what she was doing, and, spreading her hands, she murmured 'Sorry' against his lips.

'I forgive you,' he muttered, one hand cupping her bottom, and there was a hungry, carnal urgency in his gaze.

Rafe knew he couldn't wait much longer to be a part of her. His own feelings were getting dangerously out of control. He wanted to tear her clothes from her, to see the breasts that were pressing so provocatively against her bodice. Was she wearing a bra? He didn't think so. And that suspicion alone made him say thickly, 'Let's find somewhere more comfortable, shall we?'

Juliet hesitated, drawing back a little when he would have drawn her closer, and his brows came together in a frown of disbelief. 'You don't want me to touch you?' he asked, allowing one hand to slide down her throat to trace the hollow of her cleavage. 'I thought you did. Because that's what I want, Juliet.' His lips twisted. 'You have no idea how much.'

'I did. I *do*!'

Juliet spoke jerkily and he realised with some amazement that she was nervous. This woman, who'd been married for six years, was nervous. What had that bastard done to her? And he wasn't sure if he was thinking of her ex-husband or Cary…but she definitely wasn't confident about having sex with him.

Moving closer, he lifted her off her feet, and she was forced to put both legs about his waist. He was overwhelmingly aware of how it opened her to his arousal, of how it exposed her legs to her upper thighs and allowed the scent of her essence to rise seductively to his nose.

'Let's stop pretending, shall we?' he said huskily. 'You want me, and God knows, I want you. Am I right?'

'Yes. Yes.' She spoke breathily, a sexy sound that raised goose bumps on his skin. 'But—well—I'm—'

'Engaged,' said Rafe harshly. 'Yeah, I know that.'

'No.' Juliet cradled his face in his hands. 'I just wanted to warn you, I'm not—very good at this.'

Rafe blinked. 'Cary said that?'

Juliet allowed a breath to escape on a sob. 'No, David.'

'Your ex-husband.'

He didn't want to ask, but he had to. 'And Cary?'

'I haven't slept with Cary,' she admitted honestly, and Rafe wanted to howl with delight. She hesitated, and then added uncertainly, 'I don't even know if this is the right thing to do.'

'Trust me, it's the only thing to do,' said Rafe, carrying her across the sitting room and into the bedroom. He laid her on the bed, a single lamp providing the only illumination. 'Believe me, this has gone much too far now for either of us to have second thoughts.'

'Well, yes.' Juliet gazed up at him as he stood looking down at her. 'I—I'm not having second thoughts, but—'

'No buts,' he said, putting one knee on the bed beside her and allowing his hand to trail softly over her cheek. His thumb found the pulse that was racing below her ear and pressed urgently against it. 'Relax, baby. I'm not going to hurt you.'

It was incredibly difficult to take it slowly. Lying there, unconsciously seductive, she made him ache to possess her. All he really wanted to do was take off her clothes and bury his hot flesh between her legs.

Without taking his eyes from hers, he shucked off his jacket and dropped it carelessly onto the floor. He wasn't wearing a tie—which was just as well, he thought gratefully. At least the sweater allowed him to breathe.

Easing down onto one hip, he allowed his hand to move from her ear to the provocative neckline of her bodice. Tracing a line around the rim, he allowed his finger to dip beneath the cloth, discovering, as he'd anticipated, she wasn't wearing a bra.

Fortunately, there was a row of small buttons running from the neckline to her waist. His fingers fumbled, but he succeeded in opening four of the buttons, parting the lace-covered satin to reveal breasts that were full and round and already swollen with need.

'Juliet,' he said hoarsely, bending towards her. He took one ripe nipple between his teeth and heard her take a convulsive gulp of air. His tongue circled the tip, and he tasted its sweetness. Then he massaged the soft flesh with an urgency that was almost painful, before giving up and sucking the areola into his mouth.

Juliet dug her nails into the quilted coverlet, conscious that what he was doing was causing a tightening in her stomach and a throbbing awareness between her thighs. Her breasts ached and she wanted to spread her legs, and have him touch her there, too. But she couldn't tell him that, could she? She wasn't that kind of a girl.

Or was she?

Rafe lifted his head. His eyes were dark and sensual, and she shivered in anticipation of what he might do next. 'Help me,' he said, indicating the tiny buttons, and, although her fingers were slippery with perspiration, she didn't think of saying no.

The buttons opened and she lifted her hands, but instead of trying to cool her hot cheeks she caught his face between her palms and brought his mouth to hers. Her head swam as he kissed her, long, drugging kisses that made her body weak and languid with desire. She couldn't remember ever feeling this way with anyone, particularly David, and she shifted against him restlessly, trying to show him how she felt.

Rafe drew back at last, and she groaned in protest. But all he did was lay a tempting finger across her parted lips. 'We're wearing too many clothes,' he said, stroking her thigh where her dress had been pushed up in her agitation. 'Tell me, how in hell do I take this off?'

'Let me,' she said, too aroused to be reticent. Sitting up, she lifted the hem of the dress over her head. There was something liberating about not being ashamed for him to see her body, and the raw hunger in his eyes made her glad she'd shed her inhibitions.

Nevertheless, when his eyes dropped to the lacy thong that was all she was now wearing, it wasn't easy to prevent the instinctive need to cover herself. At another time, and in another place, she wouldn't have dared to be so shameless. But with Rafe's eyes upon her, she allowed herself to enjoy his admiring gaze.

However, when he hooked a finger into the waistband of the thong and tugged it lower, she couldn't deny a panicky intake of breath. And when that same finger slid down into the curls that hid her womanhood, it took every bit of control to remain where she was without crossing her legs.

But her, 'For God's sake, Rafe,' wouldn't be silenced, and Rafe slanted a look that was defined by a speculative brow.

'What?' he asked, though he knew very well why she was agitated. 'Am I doing something wrong? Perhaps you ought to show me what you like.'

'I like it all,' she confessed chokingly, closing her eyes against the hint of smugness in his face. 'Please, Rafe,' she went on, not entirely sure what she was asking for, and with a smothered oath Rafe bent forward again and buried his face between her legs.

She smelled delicious, and tasted better. The temptation was to slide his tongue into her sheath and feel her come against his mouth. But the ache between his legs forbore such generosity. He couldn't be sure he could wait so long to find his own release.

Forcing himself to be patient, he sat up and hauled off his sweater. Then, he unbuckled his belt and unfastened the button at his waist. He didn't open his zip, aware that if he did so he wouldn't be able to control his erection. He wanted her so badly and there was only so much he could take in his present state.

Juliet felt the draught as he discarded his sweater. She opened her eyes to the sight of his lean brown torso with its distinctive triangle of hair. She saw that the hair arrowed down past his flat navel, disappearing into his waistband, tempting her to discover where it had gone.

Rafe's tugging away her thong caused her to reconsider. She wasn't used to any man undressing her, had never shared the pleasure to be found in participating in her own seduction. David had expected her to take her own clothes off, even when they were on their honeymoon. And then his lovemaking had lacked any kind of foreplay. He'd taken her with as little care as he'd done everything else.

In those days Juliet had found the experience downright unpleasant, not to say painful. And later on, she supposed she'd been stiff and unresponsive whenever he'd wanted sex. She'd even wondered if that was why David had tired of her, always ready to blame herself for his mistakes.

Now, however, she knew it hadn't been all her fault. When Rafe peeled off her stockings and bestowed a trail of kisses from her instep to her inner thigh, her anticipation became intense. She could hardly wait for him to remove the other stocking and repeat the experience. She spread her legs intuitively, her palms between her thighs, holding them apart.

Rafe groaned, her innocent enticement causing an actual pain between his legs. She was so responsive, so ready for him, it was incredible. Had she any idea of what it was doing to him?

Holding her eyes with his, he quickly divested himself of his trousers and boxer shorts. Then, aware of her watching him, too, he stretched his length between her legs. 'You're very big, aren't you?' she breathed, and Rafe gave a muffled groan.

'Size isn't everything,' he whispered, trying to hang on to his sanity. But when she reached for him, he could feel his control slipping away.

Juliet was instantly aware when the smooth, rounded head of his erection probed her vagina. And, although she'd been totally relaxed a few moments before, suddenly what she was about to do didn't seem so easy, after all. Perhaps she was frigid, she thought in panic, just as David had insisted. Foreplay was one thing, but actually letting a man possess her was definitely something else.

Rafe sensed the moment when her response turned to rejection. God, he thought again, what had her ex-husband done to make her so afraid to give in? 'It's OK,' he said, putting his hand between them and finding the swollen nub that he'd tasted earlier. Massaging it gently, he felt her body relax and he took the opportunity to ease inside her. She stiffened again, but then her muscles seemed to act without her volition, expanding and enfolding him within her slick sheath.

Juliet let out a shuddering sigh as he filled her. Apprehension was giving way to anticipation and the excitement she'd felt earlier started to build once more. This wasn't David, she reminded herself, as if any reminder were necessary. This was Rafe and—God help her!—she wanted to share this pleasure with him.

'Dear God,' she moaned, giving in to her emotions. She clutched his shoulders, gazing up at him with wide, appealing eyes. 'Just—do it, hmm? Please, Rafe, I need you now.'

As if he had any choice, thought Rafe wryly. But he'd never had sex with a woman yet without giving her as much pleasure as she was giving him. 'If you're ready,' he breathed, aware that he was trembling. 'Take it easy, baby. I want to show you how good it can be.'

He moved slowly at first, withdrawing almost to the point of separation and then slowly pushing into her again. She moaned as he did so, and he bent to silence her mouth with kisses. Then, caressing her, he repeated the exercise, and felt her muscles tighten around him with obvious intent.

The response she'd shown when he'd first kissed her showed now in the urgency with which she arched against him. And, just as he'd hoped, her nervous breathing quickened to match his own. With a little cry, she wound her legs around him, and he sank so deeply into her that he was sure he'd touched her womb.

But his own needs were becoming rampant and, as she bucked and jerked against him, he let his own feelings find release. He felt the drenching heat of her orgasm only moments before he shuddered in ecstasy, spilling his seed inside her in an agony of relief…

# CHAPTER TWELVE

Bloody hell!

Rafe opened his eyes to find himself slumped on top of Juliet's supine body. He was lying between her legs, which were spread confidingly. His semi-arousal was still buried deep inside her, only needing the slightest encouragement to harden into urgent life.

Which he mustn't allow to happen!

He stifled the oath that sprang to his lips and closed his eyes against the enormity of his transgression. Despite his determination not to do so, he'd made love to his cousin's fiancée. All the contempt he'd felt for Cary's behaviour was now heaped upon his own head.

He opened his mouth to say something, to attempt some pathetic effort at an apology, and then realised Juliet was fast asleep. With one leg curled around one of his, and a hand lying limply on his thigh, she was dead to the world. Obviously exhausted, he thought guiltily, and totally unaware of the possible consequences of what they'd done.

Well, for the moment, anyway, Rafe amended, realising that happy state wouldn't last long. As soon as she opened her eyes, as soon as she discovered how he'd taken advantage of her inexperience, she'd be horrified. She might never forgive him. She might never understand how much he hated himself right now.

How could he have done such a thing? All right. She was delicious: sexy, yet strangely innocent, and oh, so very sweet. Too good for Cary, he thought with an uncharacteristic surge of arrogance. Cary would never make her happy. He was much too selfish a man to care about anybody but himself.

But was he any better?

He didn't have an answer, the question a chilling reminder that he was the one who'd seduced her, not his cousin. He might have come up here with the best of intentions. He might have meant to apologise for the way he'd behaved earlier. But what he'd actually done was take her to bed, which was the most treacherous kind of betrayal.

He had to move. Apart from anything else, he was getting a cramp in his thigh. Lying here, hoping that she'd wake up and let him do it all again, was purely evil. If he had any sense he'd get out of there, before the old lady finished her game and started wondering what had happened to them. Somehow, he couldn't see Lady Elinor approving of his actions, when she'd been at pains to ensure that Juliet and Cary shouldn't share a room. Not that he felt much loyalty towards the old lady at the moment.

Although he got to his knees without too much effort and could have easily grabbed his clothes off the floor and dressed in the sitting room, ridiculously, he lingered. He hated the thought of leaving Juliet alone. That would give her entirely the wrong impression. However base his actions had been, he still had some self-respect left.

Not that he thought she'd regard his belated concern as any kind of comfort. Salving his conscience, maybe. What the hell was he hanging about for? Absolution? It wasn't going to happen. She'd never forgive him. He might just as well grab his clothes and crawl back under his stone.

'Where are you going?'

He had one leg in his boxer shorts when Juliet's drowsy words arrested him. Quickly shoving in his other leg, he hauled them up and turned around. 'Um—I think I ought to go and see what's going on,' he muttered, wishing he had a more satisfactory explanation. He should have anticipated what he was going to say before he started getting dressed.

'Does it matter?'

Juliet pushed herself up on her elbows, the coverlet, which he'd edged over her, falling away to reveal her full, perfect breasts. Dear God, he thought, this wasn't fair. He was only human. Didn't she realise what looking at her was doing to him? Oh, yes, she must. Those sleepy eyes had dropped to the tented bulge beneath his shorts.

'In—in the normal way, no,' he said now, finding the conversation almost esoteric. 'But it's possible that—' he had to say it '—that your fiancé might be looking for you.'

'And that matters?' She was so cool, he had the feeling he'd stepped into some alternative universe. 'Oh, I get it,' she went on contemptuously, dragging the offending coverlet back into place. 'It's OK to have sex with your cousin's fiancée, so long as you don't get found out, right? God help me, that I might get the wrong idea.'

Rafe closed his eyes for a moment, wishing he'd never started this. He should have gone when he'd had half a chance. Before he put his foot in his mouth and made her think he regretted what had happened. He did, of course, though not for the reasons she thought.

All the same, she was Cary's fiancée. That should mean something to her, shouldn't it? He might think the guy was a louse, but she'd got engaged to him. Where was this crazy conversation going? However attractive the idea, he couldn't believe she was prepared to ditch Cary just because she'd had sex with him.

But he had to find out before he blew his cover completely.

'What are you saying?' he asked now, reaching for his trousers. 'Are you telling me that what we just shared changes the way you feel about Cary? We've known each other for two days, Juliet. Do you expect me to believe you've fallen madly in love with me in that time and you want to have my baby? It sounds very flattering, but are you really going to break your engagement so we can be together?'

Juliet swallowed, the whole weight of her own deception descending on her shoulders. Of course, he was right. Anything else was pure fantasy on her part. Besides, it wasn't what he wanted; that was obvious. So it was just as well she didn't have a choice.

'I—I can't,' she mumbled at last, knowing what he'd think and taking comfort from it. Far better that he believe she was a gold-digger than some pathetic twenty-something with more imagination than sense.

There was a scornful expression on his face now. 'I didn't think so,' he mocked, and she found she had to say something in her own defence.

'No, you don't understand—' she began, but Rafe ignored her.

'Don't bet on it,' he said, and paradoxically, he sounded bitter. 'I understand very well what you want and it's not the old lady's *illegitimate* grandson!'

Rafe was working when someone knocked on the windows of his studio. He'd purposely drawn the blinds at the front of the building, pushing the rear service doors wide at the back to allow the pale sunlight to seep inside. He didn't want to see anyone, he certainly didn't want to talk to anyone, and he wondered who would have the gall to disturb him at barely eight o'clock on a Sunday morning.

The irritating tapping came again, but he tried to ignore it. It could be no one he wanted to admit. According to the old lady, her guests were leaving this morning, and they'd have no reason to make a detour to Polgellin Bay.

Unless Cary had found out…

'Rafe! Rafe! Dammit, I know you're in there. Have the decency to come and open this door and let me in.'

Not Cary, then. Rafe scowled. He should have realised there was only one person who would come here to exact an explanation for the way he'd behaved the night before. And it wasn't Lady Elinor.

Throwing down the knife he'd been using to scrape a layer of paint from the canvas, he strode impatiently to the door. Yanking it open with an aggressive hand, he glared coldly at the woman who was waiting outside.

'What do you want?'

'Ooh, darling, so masterful!' Without waiting for an invitation, Liv Holderness squeezed delicately past him and into the studio. She glanced about her. 'Are you alone?'

Rafe's mouth hardened as he reluctantly closed the door. 'What do you want, Liv? I don't believe we had an appointment this morning.'

'We didn't.' But Liv wasn't perturbed by his ill humour. 'I just thought you might want to tell me what last night was all about.'

Rafe aped a look of surprise. 'Last night?' he echoed carelessly. 'Didn't you enjoy it?'

'Not as much as you did, I'll bet,' Liv flashed back, with a distinct note of resentment in her voice now. 'Why the hell didn't you tell me that you were going to be there?'

Rafe grimaced. He'd been asked that question before by someone he was trying hard not to think about, and he didn't appreciate Liv coming here and reminding him of the fact.

'I didn't know,' he said flatly. 'Believe it or not, I only received my invitation after you'd gone home.'

'Yeah, right.'

'It's true.' Rafe was struggling to keep his temper. 'Now, if that's all you've come to say—'

'It's not.' Liv drifted round the studio, picking up a photograph here, a brush there, causing Rafe no small amount of aggravation. 'Why did Lady Elinor invite you? Do you know?'

Rafe sighed. 'In polite circles, it's usual to have an equal number of men and women around the dinner table—'

'Don't patronise me, Marchese!'

'Then don't you pretend you give a damn why I was invited. I was there. That's all there is to it. If your old man didn't like what was said, take it up with Cary, not me.'

Liv seethed. 'As a matter of fact, Bobby enjoyed the evening. He and your grandmother get along very well.'

Rafe's lips twisted. 'Why wouldn't they? They've known one another for a lot of years.'

'You mean, they're nearer in age than Bobby and me.'

'I didn't say that.'

'No, but you meant it.' Liv huffed. 'Anyway, as you appear to know so much about me, why don't you tell me why I'm here?'

'Oh, no.' Rafe propped his jean-clad hips against a workbench, crossing his arms over his paint-smeared T-shirt and regarding her with mocking eyes. 'I wouldn't presume to know how your mind works.'

'Jerk!'

'I've been called worse.'

And recently, he reflected, once again stung by how easily the memory of Juliet could knock him off balance, could cause an actual knot to form in his stomach.

Liv stopped in the middle of the floor and turned to face him, and for an uncomfortable moment he thought she'd guessed what was on his mind. But all she did was stare at him mutinously before saying, 'All right. So tell me why you left the party without even joining the rest of us for a final drink?'

Rafe's jaw compressed. 'I prefer not to drink when I'm driving. I don't have a chauffeur to take me home.'

'We could have taken you home,' pointed out Liv, as if the idea had just occurred to her. 'But as you know, we didn't get the chance to offer.'

'Sorry.' But he didn't sound it.

Liv frowned. 'So why did you walk out like that? I know Lady Elinor wasn't pleased.'

'Wasn't she?' Right then, Rafe hadn't cared what Lady Elinor had thought of his behaviour. 'I was tired, OK?' he muttered irritably. 'I've had a lot of work to do lately. Not a concept I imagine you'd know anything about.'

'Yeah, yeah.' Liv wasn't impressed with his excuses. 'So your departure had nothing to do with—what's her name—Juliet?'

Rafe managed to keep his expression blank with an effort. 'Juliet?' he echoed, as if the thought was new to him. 'No. Why would it?'

'Oh, come on.' Liv was incredulous. 'You spent most of the evening with her!'

'Excuse me!' Rafe was proud of the indignation in his voice. 'We spent—perhaps—half an hour together in the library, looking at the paintings.' He frowned, pretending to consider. 'Then I think she went up to her room, and I read for a while until you'd finished your game.'

'Really?'

'Yes, really,' he said, hoping God would forgive him for the lies he was telling. It wasn't good enough to assure himself he was only doing it to protect Juliet. The truth was, he was trying to save his own skin. 'Now, if you don't mind—'

Liv heaved a deep sigh. 'So what do you think Lady Elinor had in mind when she practically pushed the two of you together? I mean, I know Cary had some sucking-up to do, but making him play cards while his fiancée was alone with another man doesn't seem fair to me.'

'When you get to know the old lady better, you'll realise that fair play's no part in her vocabulary,' said Rafe drily. 'Now, do you mind getting out of here? I've wasted enough time as it is.'

Juliet and Cary got back to London in the late afternoon. Although she knew Cary would have preferred to hang around until later in the day, she reminded him of their bargain and with ill grace he'd been forced to give in.

He had gone to see his grandmother before they left, perhaps hoping that she would agree to prevail upon Juliet to stay longer. But Hitchins had apparently cut his visit short and the old lady hadn't seemed sorry to see him go.

'It's all that bastard Rafe's fault,' Cary muttered as they accelerated up the track to the main road. 'If he hadn't had so much to say for himself last night, the old girl might have begun to see the sense in what I was saying.'

Juliet shook her head. She had a headache, actually, and she wasn't in the mood for Cary's tantrums, but that particular accusation caught her on the raw. 'If Rafe hadn't interfered, as you put it, you'd have been in even deeper trouble,' she retorted tersely. 'You're not subtle, Cary. I think it was obvious to anyone who knew about that letter from the developer that you'd read it.'

'I don't think so.'

'Well, I do.' Juliet was impatient. 'Why do you think she asked you to make up a foursome for bridge and not Rafe? She wanted to punish you, that's all. You just want to hope she's forgotten all about it by the time you make your next visit.'

Cary snorted. 'Oh, yeah. My next visit. And when I turn up without you, what do you think she's going to say about that?'

Juliet sighed. She so didn't need this. 'Cary,' she said levelly, 'you knew this was a one-time occasion. And you must have realised that Lady Elinor would be disappointed when we—well, broke up, as she'll see it.'

Cary chewed on his lower lip, cursing when another driver blew his horn at him because he'd attempted to overtake without signalling. 'I don't suppose—that is, you wouldn't consider—?'

'Repeating the exercise?' Juliet gave him a disbelieving look. 'You can't be serious!'

'Why not?' Cary warmed to the idea. 'We've pulled it off this time, haven't we? No one suspects we're not a couple, do they?'

'No.' Juliet had to concede that. 'But there's no way I'd do anything like this again.' She turned to stare blindly out of the car's window. 'I hated doing it. I felt—dirty.'

'Oh, please.' Cary was angry and he wasn't in the mood to consider her feelings. 'You enjoyed it. Don't pretend you didn't. You ought to be grateful to me. People in your situation rarely get a second chance to make something of their lives.'

Juliet gasped. 'Do you really think pretending to be your fiancée is making something of my life?'

Cary was silent for a moment and she thought he'd seen the sense of what she was saying and decided to back off. But then he spoke again.

'It doesn't have to be pretence,' he ventured carefully, and Juliet's jaw dropped.

'What?'

'Hey, don't look so shocked.' Cary's scowl was dissolving into a smile of smug anticipation. 'I'm proposing here.' He laughed delightedly. 'Dammit, why didn't I think of it before? I need a wife and you need an occupation. How convenient is that?'

# CHAPTER THIRTEEN

RAFE turned down the track towards Tregellin and drove resignedly towards the house. He hadn't visited the old lady since the disastrous evening of the dinner party over two weeks ago, and he wouldn't be here now if it weren't for Josie's frantic phone calls.

'You've got to come, Rafe,' she'd begged, just this morning. 'I'm getting really worried about her. That cold she had weeks ago has come back and she's not looking after herself the way she should.'

'So call Charteris,' said Rafe, as he'd advised before, still smarting from the shock of finding his and his mother's paintings lining the library walls, and his subsequent encounter with Juliet. The old lady had a lot to answer for and quite honestly he didn't feel any obligation to concern himself about her.

Yet here he was, just a couple of hours later, making a special trip out to Tregellin to see her. He could tell himself he was doing this for Josie until he was blue in the face, but the truth was, he did care what happened to the old lady. She was his grandmother, after all, however much they both might deplore the fact.

He parked in the usual place, and stood for a few minutes looking out at the estuary. It wasn't cold, but it was raining, a fine drizzle that soaked his hair and ran in cool rivulets over his forehead and down his cheeks. Swiping a hand across his face, he collected the things he'd brought from the back of the Land Cruiser and strode round to the rear of the house.

Josie was in the kitchen, as usual, and when Rafe opened the door Hitchins came to snuffle eagerly about his legs. 'Hey, small stuff,' he greeted the dog, depositing the bags he'd been carrying on the table and bending to pick up the Pekinese. 'What's happening?'

Josie turned from the sink, a relieved smile on her lined face. 'Thanks for coming, Rafe,' she said warmly, wiping her hands on a tea towel. She sniffed. 'We've missed you.'

'Yeah, right.' Rafe gave her an old-fashioned look before setting the little dog on the floor again. Then, ignoring Hitchins' protests, he nodded towards the bags on the table. 'I called at the supermarket on my way. I thought you might need one or two things.'

'You're too good to us!' exclaimed Josie, pulling one of the bags towards her and unloading its contents. 'Oh, smoked salmon! Perhaps I can persuade Elinor to eat a little of this.'

Rafe's brows drew together. 'She's not eating?'

'Hardly at all.' Josie exclaimed again when she found a leg of lamb and some fresh asparagus. 'She's not been right since she had that chest infection that she insisted was just a cold and I'm sure was probably flu. The cough has never properly gone away, though she won't admit it.'

Rafe felt a twinge of anxiety. 'So why haven't you called Charteris?'

'I did,' said Josie at once. 'He came, but she wouldn't see him. She told me to keep my nose out of her business. That if she needed a doctor, she'd call one for herself.'

'Crazy old woman!' Rafe blew out a weary breath. 'So that's why you've kept calling me.'

'Well, you're the only one she might listen to,' said Josie defensively. 'She thinks the world of you, Rafe; you know she does. She may not always show it, but she's very proud of you.'

Rafe scowled. 'And I suppose you knew all about those paintings,' he countered obliquely, and Josie coloured.

'I knew *of* them,' she agreed unwillingly. 'But I'd been told to say nothing to anyone, so—'

'So you kept them a secret.'

'It wasn't like that, Rafe.'

'What was it like, then? When was the old lady going to tell me about them? And why produce them that night without even a word of warning?'

'I don't know.' Clearly Josie was as perplexed as he was. 'Perhaps because you were coming to dinner.'

Rafe shook his head. 'So who put them up there? Don't tell me you were the one who moved the bookcases and hung the paintings because I won't believe you.' His eyes narrowed suspiciously. 'Was it Cary?'

'Heavens, no!' Josie was very definite about that. 'Cary knows nothing about them. I doubt he'd be very happy if he did.' She met his eyes squarely. 'She got Jem Helford to do it.' Jem and his family farmed Tregellin land further up the valley, Rafe recalled. 'He and his son came down on Saturday morning. It took them all of three hours to put everything in place.'

Rafe was stunned. 'But—why?'

'You'd have to ask Lady Elinor that.' Josie returned to unpacking the shopping. 'Oh, Rafe, we must pay you something for all this.'

'Forget it.' Rafe wasn't interested in being paid for his contribution to the household. 'Where is she? In the conservatory, as usual?'

'Actually, no, she's still in bed,' admitted Josie unhappily. 'She's taken to getting up later and later in the day. Some days, she doesn't get up at all.'

Rafe caught his breath. 'But isn't that hard on you? I mean, if you're having to run up and down stairs—'

'It does me good,' declared the housekeeper staunchly. 'And if I do go up and down the stairs, it's not for her I'm doing it. She asks for nothing. Not even her meals.'

'*Dios!*' Rafe swore. Things were so much worse than he'd expected and, as usual, he felt guilty for staying away.

With a rueful look in Josie's direction, he left the kitchen, striding swiftly across the hall before vaulting up the stairs, two at a time. If he gave any thought to the last time he'd climbed these stairs—and with what purpose—he didn't acknowledge it. That was just something else the old lady could blame him for and he'd had enough of being everyone's whipping boy.

Even so, when he reached Lady Elinor's bedroom door he paused for a moment to get his breath back. It wouldn't do for her to think he'd been worried about her. Then, after raking back his hair with an impatient hand, he tapped sharply on the panels.

There was silence for a few moments, and then a rather frail voice called, 'Come in, Raphael. If you must.'

Rafe stifled the resentment her words inspired and plastered a smile on his face. She'd evidently heard the car and she was just trying to get a rise out of him, but it wasn't going to happen. Pushing open the door, he sauntered into the room. 'Hello, old lady,' he greeted her, with similar irreverence. 'Do you know what time it is?'

He spoke carelessly, but the old lady's appearance shocked him. She looked so pale, her hair, which had always seemed more black than white, a loose grey curtain about her thin shoulders. Lying back against her white pillows, she looked every one of her almost eighty years and Rafe's stomach took a decided plunge.

'I believe it's after twelve o'clock,' she declared at last, and there was a reassuring trace of impatience in her voice. 'What's it to you, Raphael? You don't seem to care what happens to me these days.'

Rafe bit back the retort that first sprang to his lips and instead said mildly, 'That is not true, old lady. Anyway, it cuts both ways. Why didn't you let me know if you wanted to see me?'

'What? And have you tell me you didn't have time to waste coming here to see an old woman you both hate and despise?' Lady Elinor tilted her chin. 'I think not.'

Rafe sighed. 'I neither hate nor despise you,' he muttered

heavily. 'Whatever—or should I say whoever—gave you that idea?'

Lady Elinor turned her head aside to stare out of her window. 'What else was I supposed to think when you haven't said a word about the little exhibition I arranged for you? Indeed, it seems obvious to me that you were furious at my little deception and that's why you've stayed away. Not to mention the insulting way you walked out of here two weeks ago, without even acknowledging my kindness for inviting you.'

'Your kindness?' Despite the curb he'd put on his temper, Rafe found that was one word too far. 'There was nothing kind about confronting me with paintings I'd thought had been sold years ago. And how long have you had those paintings of my mother's? You let me think everything of hers had been either lost or destroyed when she died.'

'When she committed suicide, you mean?' Lady Elinor said flatly, stunning Rafe into silence. 'Oh, Raphael, you don't allow for anyone's vulnerabilities, do you?' Her voice shook a little now. 'How do you think I felt when I found out what had happened? Christina was my daughter. I loved her dearly. Yet she abandoned me to take up with some itinerant Italian labourer, who treated her so badly she was forced to run away.'

Rafe blinked. 'That's not true!'

'I'm afraid it is.'

'No. I mean…' He stared at her with tortured eyes. 'I know my father treated her badly sometimes. I remember the rows they used to have, the arguments that went on for hours. But my mother didn't commit suicide. She—she fell. From a hotel balcony.'

Lady Elinor turned to look at him again. 'That was the story I chose to tell everyone,' she said wearily. 'You were a sensitive child. I didn't know what kind of damage hearing your mother had killed herself might do to you. For years, I thought I might never tell you. But you're a man now, and I can't carry the burden alone any longer.'

Rafe shook his head. Then, dragging a chair from beneath the

windows, he swung it round and straddled it to face her. 'So,'
he said harshly. 'Tell me what really happened. Did she kill
herself because of my father? Is that what you're trying to say?'

'No. No.' Lady Elinor sighed. 'Nothing so dramatic, Raphael.
Christina had a little money of her own, so she took you and fled
to Switzerland.' She paused. 'Regrettably, she started drinking.
She did very little painting after she left Italy, and I'm fairly sure
her money was getting short. Then, one night, she climbed up
onto the rail surrounding the balcony of your hotel room. And,
according to witnesses, she simply stepped off into space.'

Rafe's lips felt dry. 'So she did fall?'

'Yes, she fell.' The old lady sounded bleak, however. 'But
there seems little doubt of what she'd had in mind. She'd written
me a letter, you see. It arrived in England two days later. In it
she asked if, in the event of her death, I would bring you back
to England and give you a home.'

Rafe groaned, covering his head with one arm, burying his
face against his sleeve. 'So that's why you never liked me.'

'Never liked you?' Lady Elinor sat up straight. 'I don't know
what you're talking about, Raphael. I love you. I've always loved
you, right from the first moment I saw you in that *kinderstube* in
Interlaken.' She sniffed, reaching for her handkerchief, and Rafe
was amazed to see that there were tears in her eyes now. 'They'd
put you with the younger children, but I recognised you instantly.
You were so tall; so handsome; so like Christina, I wanted to weep.'
She sniffed again. 'I never even thought of trying to contact your
father. As far as I was concerned, you were Christina's son, my
grandson, and that was all that mattered.' She made a rocking
movement of her hand. 'Later on, as I believe I told you, I made
enquiries and discovered your father had been killed in a car
accident soon after Christina left him. It has crossed my mind that
that might have been what drove her to do what she did, but we'll
never know for sure. The important thing, so far as I was concerned,
was that she'd turned to me in her hour of need. You were here, at
Tregellin, and whatever you think, I have never regretted it.'

Rafe didn't know what to think. When he'd driven here this morning, he'd had no idea the old lady was going to drop such a bombshell. Yet it made more sense; now that he was older, he could see that. His mother had been a passionate, emotional woman. It was fitting, somehow, that her death should be a passionate and emotional one, too.

'What are you thinking?'

Lady Elinor was regarding him anxiously now, and Rafe folded his arms across the back of the chair and rested his chin on his wrist. 'I'm thinking you've had it pretty tough yourself, old lady,' he admitted honestly. 'It can't have been easy losing both your children before their fortieth birthdays.'

Lady Elinor stifled what sounded suspiciously like a sob. 'Yes, Charles' death, too, was a devastating blow. For years I'd lived alone, and suddenly I had two young boys to care for.' She grimaced rather wryly. 'But, do you know, I do believe you and Cary kept me sane?'

Rafe frowned. 'OK. So why did you let me think that everything that belonged to my mother had been either lost or destroyed?'

The old lady sighed and sank back against her pillows. 'It was easier that way.'

'Easier?'

'Easier for me,' admitted Lady Elinor regretfully. 'I'm afraid it took me many years to forgive Christina for what she'd done. Having her child was one thing. Having her paintings around me—the thing that had driven her from me—was something else.'

'So?'

'So I had them all packed up and stored in the attic. Along with those early paintings of yours that I'd had a third party obtain for me.'

'The solicitor from Bodmin.'

'The solicitor from Bodmin,' she agreed, pressing her lips together for a moment. 'I knew you'd never forgive me, so I didn't tell you what I'd done.'

Rafe shook his head. 'But why did you do it?'

'Can't you guess?' Lady Elinor was succinct. 'I thought if I bought your paintings, they wouldn't be seen by other collectors. I'd already lost my daughter because of her love of art. I was so afraid I was going to lose you in the same way.'

Rafe stared at her for a long moment, and then, discarding the chair, he crossed the room to sit down on the bed beside her. 'You'll never lose me, old lady,' he said gruffly, gathering her frail body up into his arms and pressing her face into his shoulder. 'You may be a cantankerous old bird, but you're my old bird, and that's what matters to me.'

Lady Elinor yielded against him, but only for a few moments. Then, with a briskness that belied her age, she urged him away. 'I was right,' she said, though her voice was unaccountably thick, 'you're just like your mother. I can't do with all this emotion. I'm a plain woman. I say what I think.'

Rafe's smile was gentle. 'Treat 'em mean and keep 'em keen, yeah?'

'I don't know what you mean.' But her voice was definitely gaining in strength and there was a touch of colour in her cheeks. 'Anyway, let's talk about something else, shall we? Have you forgiven me for making you spend the evening with Juliet?'

Rafe got up then, pacing restlessly about the bedroom, not prepared to suffer the old lady's scrutiny at such close hand. 'What's to forgive?' he said at last, and he was proud of the indifference in his tone. 'I dare say it got up Cary's nose though.'

'Do you think so?' Lady Elinor was surprisingly restrained. 'Well, maybe because it was you, yes. But didn't you think Cary was amazingly cavalier about his fiancée?'

Rafe turned to frown at her. 'Cavalier?'

'Yes.' The old lady pleated the hem of the linen sheet. 'It made me wonder exactly what their engagement is all about.' She paused. 'Juliet left your mother's ring behind, you know?'

Rafe hadn't known. But then, how could he? This was his first visit to Tregellin since that fateful weekend.

'I expect Cary wants to buy her a ring,' he said offhandedly, not allowing himself to read anything into Juliet's gesture. 'Anyway, you'll be pleased to have it back.'

'Hmm.' Lady Elinor didn't sound particularly convinced. 'What did you think of her?'

'Juliet?' His stomach tightened convulsively.

'Who else?' There was a touch of asperity in her voice now. 'Josie's convinced the engagement won't last. She thinks Juliet has more in common with you.'

'You're joking!'

'No, I'm not joking.' Lady Elinor's mouth was tight. 'Josie's entitled to her opinion, isn't she?'

'Well, yes, but—'

'You mean, you've never thought of her in that way?' the old lady probed and Rafe blew out a frustrated breath.

'Of course I've thought of Juliet in that way,' he muttered, deciding there was no point in denying it. 'She's a beautiful woman. A man would have to be blind not to notice it.'

'And you're not blind, are you, Raphael?' Lady Elinor remarked drily. 'Not if half the stories I've heard about you are true.'

Rafe scowled. 'You shouldn't believe all you hear.'

'Oh, I don't.' The old lady nodded. 'But I have to say, on this occasion, I do agree with Josie. Juliet is far too good for Cary. Let's hope she realises it in time, hmm?'

# CHAPTER FOURTEEN

THE letter was lying in her mailbox when she got home from work.

Juliet wasn't used to getting mail—unless it was a bill, of course—but the fine vellum of the envelope ensured it wasn't one of those. And it was her name that was printed in black typescript, her address correctly delineated, even down to the number of her apartment.

With a shrug, she put the letter into her bag and started up the stairs, wondering if it had anything to do with David. But her ex-husband never contacted her and he was unlikely to have come back to England. With a possible case for the fraudulent transfer of funds hanging over his head, she doubted—indeed, she hoped—that she'd never see him again.

Her apartment was on the second floor, and in the small entry she slipped off her jacket and kicked off her high heels. It would be July next week and the apartment was airless. Crossing to the windows, she released the security catch and pushed up the sash. Then, after taking a breath of cooler air, she turned back into the room.

She needed a shower, she thought, glancing down at her skirt with its ugly smear of tomato ketchup. Parents really shouldn't let children take hamburgers on the bus, she thought ruefully. Apologising when your six-year-old had dropped a burger into your neighbour's lap was not quite good enough.

She had a hard enough time of it as it was, keeping her clothes neat and clean without spending too much on them. But working in a small boutique required her to look reasonably smart at all times. Granted, the shortness of her hems and the amount of cleavage the management expected her to show weren't exactly high fashion. But the shop's clientele had certain expectations, and Juliet was so grateful to have a job, she hadn't been prepared to argue.

Not that she intended to remain at the boutique any longer than she had to. She was taking a course in computing and office management at evening class with a view to finding more interesting employment before the end of the year. She was optimistic of achieving her goal. Her tutor, a retired computer programmer, had said she had a real aptitude for the work.

It had been a struggle. Particularly as she'd refused to take the money Cary had offered her after their return from Cornwall. He'd thought she was a fool, but she'd felt bad enough as it was without taking what she suspected was Lady Elinor's money. By pawning her wrist-watch, she'd got by, and the reference she had accepted from him had been enough for Sandra Sparks, the boutique's manageress.

But now, she couldn't put off opening the letter any longer. Finding a knife in the alcove that served as both kitchen and dining area, she ran it under the flap and slit it across. Then, with what she recognised were delaying tactics, she put the knife back in the drawer before pulling out the single sheet of paper that was inside.

She saw at once that it was from a firm of solicitors in Bodmin. *Bodmin!* Her heart skipped a beat and the hand holding the sheet of paper trembled as she read on.

The letter advised her of the death—*the death!*—of Lady Elinor Margaret Daniels of Tregellin House, Tregellin, Cornwall, and invited her to the reading of Lady Elinor's will, which would take place on Monday, July 2nd, after the funeral service and internment at St Mawgan's Church in the village of Tregellin.

Juliet sank down onto the nearest chair. She was feeling sick and shaky, and she stared at the letter blindly, hardly able to believe what she'd just read. Lady Elinor—that bright, indomitable old lady—was dead. Dear lord, how must Rafe be feeling? He'd loved his grandmother. That had been evident. And now Cary would inherit Tregellin and the old house would be sold.

Curiously, she didn't feel much compassion for Cary. It had been obvious from the start where his sympathies lay. He wanted to sell Tregellin; to realise its potential for development. He'd probably already started planning what he was going to do once probate had been granted.

But Rafe was different. Although he'd never said as much, she'd sensed he loved Tregellin, too. Certainly he'd defended it when Cary had made his pitch for selling the land. But now that Lady Elinor was gone, there was nothing to stop Cary from doing as he liked.

Oh, Rafe…

Unable to sit still, Juliet got to her feet again and paced about the apartment. She'd tried so hard not to think about him since she'd got back to London, and she'd almost succeeded. Time was a great healer. She'd learned that both when her father died and when David had betrayed her. She'd hoped that in time she'd be able to think about Rafe without emotion, but she feared that situation was some way off yet.

Besides, it had probably been foolish to imagine she could dismiss what had happened without heartache, even if the memory of that whole weekend had assumed the aspect of a dream. It had been real enough, she acknowledged. It was she who'd made it illusory. Pretending to be Cary's fiancée; deceiving all of them, but most particularly Rafe.

She shook her head. And now Lady Elinor had died, possibly still believing she and Cary were engaged to be married. Why else would she have been invited to the reading of her will? Juliet felt so ashamed; so deceitful. She had no right to be involved in Lady Elinor's affairs.

She looked again at the letter. She should write back to this solicitor—Mr Peter Arnold—and explain that she and Cary were no longer seeing one another. No longer! Her lips twisted. They'd never been seeing one another. But that would take too much explanation, and she wasn't actually sure if what they'd done was entirely legal.

She bit her lip and frowned down at the sheet of paper. Whatever Cary had or hadn't said, this was a family occasion, and she had no part in it. She should simply write a polite little note to these solicitors, expressing her condolences to the family, and excuse herself on the grounds that she couldn't get the time off from her job. It was probably true, anyway. She hadn't been at the boutique long enough to qualify for special treatment.

Then, when the tears welled up in her eyes, she realised she didn't want to refuse the invitation. She'd liked Lady Elinor. She'd liked her a lot. She'd been kind to Juliet, offering her the ring and all. She was really sorry the old lady had died. And she would like to pay her last respects in person.

The knowledge that, if she did go to the funeral, she'd see Rafe again wasn't an issue, she told herself. Since she hadn't heard from him since she got back, it was obvious that what had happened had not meant as much to him as it had to her. Besides, he'd know her now for the liar she was. Cary couldn't have kept up his deception. Not without her participation.

She was still undecided what she was going to do when she went to bed that night. Whatever way she looked at it, her presence would be an intrusion into the family's grief. Poor Josie must be distraught, she thought. She and Lady Elinor had been together for so long. And when Tregellin was sold, she'd lose her home as well. Juliet didn't fool herself that Cary would give the old housekeeper's needs a thought.

After a restless night, she decided to ring the solicitor in Bodmin. She wanted to explain to him that she and Cary were no longer 'involved' and that, although she'd like to come to the funeral, she'd prefer not to attend the reading of the will.

She had to wait until her morning coffee break to ring the solicitor's office. And then she was put on hold for several minutes before a man came on the line. 'Ms Lawrence?' he asked, and she confirmed her identity. 'Oh—well, what can I do for you? I'm afraid my father's busy with another client, but I'm Stephen Arnold, his son.'

Juliet stifled a sigh and briefly explained why she was ringing. She didn't go into details, but she let it be known that she had no connection to the Daniels family any more. 'I'm hoping to attend the funeral,' she went on, 'but I'll return to London as soon as it's over. I'm afraid my being invited to attend the reading of the will was a mistake.'

'Oh, no.' Stephen Arnold was very definite about that. 'You are one of the beneficiaries, Ms Lawrence. Your inclusion was quite deliberate, I can assure you.'

Juliet's breath caught in her throat. 'No—that's not possible. I'm not a member of the family.'

'My father knows that, Ms Lawrence. But Lady Elinor was a very determined lady. When she made this clause in your favour, she told him you were a young lady she'd come to like and admire.'

'Admire!'

Juliet wanted to die of shame. If only she'd told the old lady the truth; if only she'd had the guts to refuse Cary's money before it was too late. As it was, the fraud they'd established had been perpetuated. And now that Lady Elinor was gone, there was no way she could make amends.

'So you will be present on Monday afternoon?' Stephen Arnold prompted pleasantly. 'I know my father is looking forward to meeting you.'

Really? Juliet didn't say the word out loud, but she must have made a suitable response, because a few moments later the phone went dead and she was forced to return it to its cradle.

'Problems?'

Juliet was still sitting staring at the phone when Sandra Sparks came into the office, where she'd been making the call.

The young manageress regarded her newest employee sympathetically, and Juliet gave a weary shake of her head.

'You could say that.' She paused. 'Is it all right if I take next Monday off? I've got to go to a funeral.'

Sandra frowned. 'A family member, is it?'

Juliet suddenly realised the difficulty. 'No.'

'Oh, dear.' Sandra sighed. 'Staff are only supposed to take time off to attend family funerals. Compassionate leave, so to speak. I'm really sorry, Juliet, but I can't allow you to go.'

Juliet stared at her. 'But I have to go!' she exclaimed. 'I've— promised. It's important to me, Sandra, or I wouldn't ask.'

Sandra sighed again. 'Where is this funeral? Perhaps I could allow you to slip out for a couple of hours. You'd have to keep it quiet, of course. If it gets around that I'm a soft touch, all the girls will use it as an excuse.'

Juliet bent her head. 'A couple of hours wouldn't do it, I'm afraid. The funeral's in Cornwall. At a place called Tregellin. Lady—Lady Elinor Daniels is—*was*—someone I've known for a long time.' Which was only a slight exaggeration of the truth.

'*Lady* Elinor Daniels?' Sandra was obviously impressed. 'So how do you know her? Was she your godmother or something?'

'It's a long story. She knew my father,' said Juliet flatly. 'Just recently—just recently, I stayed with her. It would mean a lot to me to be able to say goodbye.'

Sandra was weakening. Juliet could see it. 'And you would only need the one day?'

Juliet nodded. 'I'd go down on Sunday and come back Monday evening,' she said, hoping it would work out. 'I'm sure there must be trains. It's the holiday season, after all.'

So, they were still together.

Cary had said they were, but Rafe hadn't wanted to believe him. Certainly the last time Cary had visited their grandmother, Juliet hadn't been with him. He'd made some excuse about her having a cold and not wanting to infect Lady Elinor, but Rafe had been suspicious. Even if he hadn't had enough conviction to check up on her himself.

Which was just as well, in the circumstances, he thought grimly, his eyes flickering over the couple who stood at the opposite side of the grave. But that didn't stop him from feeling angry. So angry that he felt as if he was choking on it. And he didn't even want to explore why that should be so.

Perhaps he'd hoped that she wouldn't come, that some small shred of decency would prevent her from appearing at his grandmother's graveside as if she had a right to be there. Had she no shame? She'd been engaged to Cary when he'd made love to her, and, despite that air of assumed innocence, she still was. How could she stand there, beside Cary, looking as if butter wouldn't melt in her mouth, when he knew damn well how hot she was?

His teeth ground together and Josie, who was hanging on to his arm, gave him a curious look. Her eyes were still swollen from the tears she'd cried since Lady Elinor passed away, but they were as sharp as ever and far too shrewd.

'What's wrong?'

Rafe shook his head. 'What could be wrong?' he demanded bitterly. 'The old lady's dead and Cary can't wait to get his hands on Tregellin. Everything's peachy.'

Josie sighed and patted his arm. 'You shouldn't jump to conclusions, Rafe,' she said softly. 'Your grandmother might have been old, but she was nobody's fool. Give her a little credit, won't you? I'd have thought finding out about those paintings would have taught you that she had her secrets, too.'

'Too?' Rafe cast a wary glance in her direction. 'I've got no secrets. My life's an open book.'

'Is it?' Rafe wasn't sure, but he thought Josie cast a thoughtful look in Juliet's direction. 'Ah, well, we'll know soon enough. When Mr Arnold reads the will.'

Rafe scowled. He'd have just as soon not attended the reading of the old lady's will. There was so much hypocrisy in standing around, waiting to see how much his grandmother had left. Cary would be there, and Juliet, apparently. Scavengers, both of them, he thought savagely. They deserved each other.

Even so, he couldn't prevent images of the last time he'd seen Juliet from filling his mind. He might not want to remember how shamelessly beautiful she'd looked when she'd told him she had no intention of breaking her engagement, but he was powerless to stop it. And in the three months since she'd left Tregellin, he'd lived a celibate lifestyle. He'd never been precisely promiscuous, but he'd never felt such an aversion to having sex with another woman before.

Perhaps that was what was wrong with him, he reflected tensely. It wasn't just seeing Juliet and Cary together. It was the fact that it had been several months since he'd got laid. As soon as this pitiful charade was over he was going to drive into Bodmin, get a skinful of beer and find himself a woman. Any woman would do, he told himself. Just as long as she could drive all thoughts of Juliet out of his head.

Juliet, meanwhile, was not unaware of Rafe glowering at her from across the gravesite. If she'd ever had any doubts about his feelings, she could see now how foolish she'd been. He resented her being there. That was blatantly obvious. Their sexual encounter was something he'd sooner forget.

OK, she was guilty of not telling him the truth about her and Cary when he'd asked her about her engagement. But she'd been in a cleft stick, aware that anything she said would reflect on Cary in the most unfavourable way. Surely the fact that she and Cary had—as he would see it—broken up as soon as they'd got back to London should have told him something. If he'd wanted to hear it, of course, she appended. Which, judging by his present attitude, he evidently hadn't.

She sighed, and Cary glanced at her. 'It'll soon be over,' he said. 'Then we can get back to the house.'

For 'get back to the house' read 'hear what Lady Elinor's will has to say', Juliet thought bitterly. She doubted anyone around the gravesite had any illusions as to why Cary was really here.

The last words of the interment were said and Rafe bent to drop a handful of soil onto the brass-bound casket. 'Sleep well, old lady,' he said in an undertone, before turning and striding back to where the cars were waiting.

Juliet saw him go, but when she would have hurried after him Cary caught her arm. 'Where are you going?'

Juliet snatched her arm away. 'Is it any of your business?' Since she'd arrived at Tregellin that morning he'd adopted a very proprietary air towards her, almost as if he were responsible for her invitation. Which she knew, most definitely, was not the case. 'I'll see you back at the house.'

Cary scowled. 'You're hoping to talk to him, aren't you?' he demanded angrily. 'Well, forget it, love. I'm the one you should be seen with, not him.'

'Why?'

'Because—because they still think we're a couple,' muttered Cary, obviously with some reluctance. And at her look of horror, 'What was I supposed to say? Did you want the old girl to find out I'd been lying to her?'

Juliet couldn't believe her ears. 'So you think the only reason I've been invited here is because of you?'

'Looks that way.' Cary was smug now.

'I don't believe it. I don't believe you.' She gazed at him with contempt. 'Well, you'd better tell everyone that our "engagement" is over. And don't follow me, Cary. Not unless you want me to broadcast the fact that there never was an engagement in the first place.'

Rafe saw her coming. He was leaning against the bonnet of one of the funeral cars, waiting for Josie to pay her last respects and join him. He'd intended to drive his own car to the service, but Josie had begged him to accompany her in one of the limousines. 'People will expect it,' she said. And he knew by 'people', she meant Peter Arnold and his son.

He felt the muscles of his face tightening as Juliet stopped beside him. He wasn't going to speak first, he thought childishly.

As far as he was concerned, he wanted no empty sympathy from her. Despite the fact of what being this close to her again was doing to his equilibrium.

She looked so innocent, he acknowledged bitterly. Although Lady Elinor wouldn't have wanted anyone to wear mourning, Juliet's pale grey suit and salmon-pink top showed just the right amount of respect. High heels gave her the extra height so she only had to tilt her chin a little to look up at him, her silky hair a precarious knot on top of her head.

'Hi,' she said, when he didn't speak, and Rafe unfolded his arms and inclined his head politely. 'I just wanted to say how sorry I am that Lady Elinor has passed away. She—she seemed so strong, somehow. So vital. I was shocked when I got Mr Arnold's letter.'

That got his attention. 'Arnold wrote to you?'

'That's right.'

'Why?'

'I don't know why.' Juliet felt the same sense of uncertainty she'd experienced when she'd first opened the letter. 'I did phone him. I thought it must be a mistake.' She moistened her lips. 'He said—or rather his son said—it wasn't.'

Rafe's brows descended. 'You're telling me Cary didn't mention his grandmother's illness?' His lips twisted. 'Forgive me, but even for Cary that seems a little unlikely.'

'How could he?' Juliet twisted the strap of her handbag. This was harder than she'd thought. 'How could Cary tell me? I haven't seen him since we got back from Cornwall three months ago.'

Rafe couldn't hide his anger. 'Do you expect me to believe that?' he snarled. 'What kind of an engagement do you have? An open one, obviously. But pretending you haven't seen him—'

'I haven't!' Juliet looked up at him with frustrated eyes. 'Oh, what's the use? I knew you wouldn't believe me. Cary's filled your head with so many lies, anything I say is just so much hot air.'

'Hot, certainly,' said Rafe provokingly, and Juliet gave him an angry glare.

'Oh, believe what you like,' she said, turning away. 'You will anyway. If you must know, there never was an engagement. Cary persuaded me to act as his girlfriend, just for that one weekend. It was never intended to be an engagement. That was Cary's doing. I agreed because I needed the money. And he promised he'd give me a reference so I could get a proper job—'

Rafe stared at her incredulously. 'Cary paid you!'

'He was supposed to, but—in the end I wouldn't take his money.' She shook her head. 'After—after meeting Lady Elinor, I felt such a—such a—'

'Bitch?'

'—a fraud,' she amended huskily, feeling the hot sting of tears behind her eyes, but Rafe wasn't impressed.

'My God,' he said contemptuously, 'no wonder you were so anxious when I asked you if you were going to break your engagement. The old lady would have kicked both of you out if she'd known what a pair of liars you were.'

Juliet sighed. 'Do you think I don't know that?'

'So aren't you ashamed?'

'Oh, God, of course I'm ashamed!' Juliet caught her breath. 'But I couldn't let Cary down, could I? Can't you see that?'

'All I can see is a greedy, grasping female, with an eye to the main chance,' retorted Rafe coldly. 'But hey, this isn't the time to be breaking your engagement, lady. Not when Cary is just about to scoop the pool.'

Juliet felt chilled. 'I've told you, there was no engagement!'

'Then perhaps this is the time to start thinking about one,' he taunted, and she wondered how she could have ever thought that they might have a future together.

'Do you think I care about the money?' she asked bitterly, and Rafe lifted his shoulders in a careless gesture.

'You did.'

'No!' She was aware of the other mourners leaving the grave-side now, but she had to try and make him understand. 'I was practically destitute. I needed a few pounds, that's all. Just a few pounds to tide me over until I could find employment. But I've got a job now, so I don't need anybody's charity. And whatever you think, nothing—*nothing*—would persuade me to marry Cary Daniels. I don't even like him.' She swayed a little, but when he tried to help her she flinched away. 'As soon as this is over, I'm going home.'

# CHAPTER FIFTEEN

THE train from Bodmin to Paddington rattled over the points and then resumed its steady rhythm. It wasn't full. Despite the season, the lateness of the hour had apparently put off all but the most determined travellers. Couples with children tended to prefer the earlier trains, although there were one or two toddlers sleeping on their parents' knees.

Juliet had been lucky enough to find a corner seat. Although there'd been a reserved ticket attached to it, no one had claimed the seat before the train left the station. In consequence, she wasn't obliged to make conversation with her neighbours. Tilting her head against the pane, she closed her eyes and tried to sleep.

But she'd known that would be impossible before she even tried it. Her mind was too full of the events and images of the day to find any escape in sleep. Even now, it was difficult to assimilate what had happened. Evidently Cary felt the same. Yet despite his disappointment, he had apparently decided to spend another night at the house.

Not that she cared what Cary did, one way or the other. Discovering he'd continued to deceive Rafe about their relationship had destroyed what little liking she'd had left. Her only consolation was that he hadn't deceived his grandmother. Lady Elinor had made it her business to learn everything there was to know about her grandson and his 'girlfriend'. According to Mr

Arnold, Cary's relationship with the stripper from the casino where he worked had not gone unremarked.

Cary had tried to deny it. He'd even had the nerve to appeal to Juliet to help him out of the pit he'd dug for himself. But Juliet wanted nothing more to do with him, and had said so. And then the surprise Mr Arnold had delivered to her had caused Cary to accuse her of ingratiating herself with his grandmother for her own ends.

It had all been rather unpleasant and Juliet hadn't been able to look in Rafe's direction. She was sure he must think the same as Cary. That she'd somehow hinted at her financial situation and Lady Elinor had decided to help her out. It wasn't true. She'd never discussed her finances with his grandmother. But who would believe her now?

Anyway, it appeared that Lady Elinor had left her the three rings she'd shown them from her jewellery box; the rings she'd offered Juliet to choose from that afternoon at Tregellin. There was the ruby ring, which had been Rafe's mother's, the emerald dress ring and the diamond solitaire. They were Juliet's now to wear or sell, as she pleased.

Juliet was both touched and embarrassed. The rings were heirlooms, all of them, and she felt she had no right to remove them from the estate. But Mr Arnold insisted that the codicil to the will and been added just weeks ago, at Lady Elinor's specific request, that she'd wanted her to have the rings with her blessing.

Josie, who was sitting beside her in the library, where the reading of the will was taking place, squeezed her hand. 'Elinor liked you,' she said in an undertone. 'She wanted you to have something of hers to keep.'

And Juliet knew that, whatever happened, she would keep the rings; two of them, at least. The ruby, which had been Rafe's mother's, she intended to return to him after she got back to London. That way, there'd be no chance of him throwing it back in her face.

Further bequests followed, to people Juliet hadn't heard of, and the doctor, whom she had. And Josie, of course. The housekeeper was given a lump sum of one hundred thousand pounds, which brought a gasp of disbelief from Cary, and the title to a small cottage in the grounds, where she could live when she retired.

Even Rafe looked surprised at Josie's good fortune, but unlike Cary he was the first to applaud the old lady's decision. 'You deserve it,' he said, his gaze skimming Juliet's flushed face before moving on to the housekeeper. 'Without your care and support, she'd never have been able to keep this place going.'

'And that's a reason to reward her?' Cary was scathing. He scowled. 'I knew the old girl wasn't as hard-up as she pretended to be. But giving away a hundred K! That's ridiculous!'

'It was her money, Mr Daniels, to do with as she wished.' The solicitor had regarded him with a reproving gaze. 'But now we come to the distribution of the bulk of Lady Elinor's estate. I suggest you allow me to proceed.'

That had silenced him, but Juliet shivered now as she recalled the events that had followed. No one had been prepared for the news Mr Arnold had to relate, but she supposed they should have had some intimation when he'd announced that Cary had been left two hundred thousand pounds in treasury bonds. The remainder of the estate—including the house, the farms surrounding it and the contents of a safety-deposit box lodged with her bank in Bodmin—had been left to Lady Elinor's eldest grandson.

'But that's me!' Cary exclaimed, confused by the distinction between his bequest and the latter designation. 'I'm the old girl's only legitimate grandson. Rafe…' He cast his cousin a scornful look. 'He's a bastard, in more ways than one.'

'I'm afraid not.' Before the solicitor spoke again, Juliet glimpsed the pain that briefly crossed Rafe's face. But then, Mr Arnold extracted another envelope from his briefcase and handed it to Rafe with a curious smile. 'This is yours, I believe. Your grandmother asked me to give it to you with her apologies.'

'What is it?' Cary demanded, his face red and angry, a mixture of fury and apprehension that things weren't as simple as he'd believed.

Rafe ignored him, drawing the document out amid the hushed silence that had fallen over the room. Then, his expression warned them all of the shock he'd just received. His skin had become so pale that Juliet half expected him to collapse. But Mr Arnold took it upon himself to explain that it was Rafe's parents' marriage certificate. A certificate that had been dated some thirty-two years ago, before Rafe was born.

Of course, Cary hadn't believed it. He'd been incensed, snatching the certificate out of Rafe's nerveless grasp and brandishing it in his face while he'd called him every offensive name he could think of. 'This is a fake,' he'd snarled. 'The old girl was off her rocker!' He'd swung round on Mr Arnold. 'Who did she get to forge this for her? No, don't bother to answer that. Marchese probably made it himself.'

'It's no fake,' the solicitor had informed him smoothly, taking the document out of his hand before any damage was done. Then he'd turned to the other man. 'I'm sorry, Rafe. I know she wanted to tell you before this, but she was afraid if she did she'd lose you. Tregellin's yours now. It's her gift to you. I think you'll find she's had this in mind all along.'

Juliet found her eyes were filled with tears now. Dear Lady Elinor, she thought. You knew which of your grandsons cared about Tregellin and which didn't. She supposed it was hard on Cary, bearing in mind that he'd expected to inherit the estate. But if he had, he'd have had no hesitation about selling it. And, although Rafe wasn't going to find it easy, she knew he'd do everything in his power to keep his legacy intact.

Juliet herself had slipped away while Mr Arnold was explaining the legalities to Rafe and Josie. She wasn't needed any longer and she had no intention of getting embroiled in Cary's vengeful schemes. She wouldn't put it past him to try and contest the will, if he could. But she had the feeling Mr Arnold was more than a match for him.

It was a couple of days later when she saw Cary again. She was coming out of the boutique at lunchtime when he accosted her. 'Hey,' he said, catching her arm and swinging her round to face him. 'Where did you get to the other afternoon? I thought you must be taking a last look at the property, but although I searched the place I couldn't find you.'

'Oh—I— It wasn't my place to be there,' said Juliet uncomfortably. And then, frowning, 'How did you know where to find me today?'

'Well, I went to the apartment,' said Cary at once. 'And some old lady told me you'd got a job at a boutique in town. She said she thought the place was called Close To You or something, and, as luck would have it, I remembered a place called Close-Up, and here you are.'

Juliet pulled a face. She guessed it must be Mrs Heaton who had given him the information. The old lady hadn't been well lately and, since Juliet had been going into town every day, she'd done a little shopping for her. Naturally, Mrs Heaton had asked where she was working and Juliet had seen no harm in telling her.

Now, though, she wished she'd been a little more vague about her employer. She couldn't imagine why Cary might want to seek her out, but her instincts told her it wasn't just to be polite. 'So what do you want?' she asked, aware that she didn't sound exactly friendly. 'I only get half an hour for lunch. I've got to be back at half-past one.'

Cary pulled a face. 'Hey, is that any way to greet your ex-fiancé?' he demanded.

'You're not my ex-fiancé,' said Juliet tersely. 'Come on, Cary, what do you want?'

Cary scowled. 'Let me buy you lunch. Then I'll tell you.' He lifted a hand as she started to protest. 'All right, just a sandwich. There's a coffee shop across the road.'

'I know that.' It was where Juliet occasionally spent her lunchtimes. If she'd brought her college books to work she sometimes spent half an hour studying for her course. Thankfully, today she hadn't brought the books with her. She didn't want Cary seeing them and ridiculing her efforts.

'OK, then.' Cary put a hand on her bare arm. 'Let's go.'

It was easier to go with him than to argue. Staff weren't encouraged to invite friends or relations to visit the shop. The last thing she needed was for Cary to kick up a fuss just outside the door and cause Sandra to come and see what was going on. But she yanked her arm out of his grasp before they crossed the street.

'You're not wearing one of the rings,' Cary observed, after she'd accepted a coffee. 'I don't know whether you realise it, but those rings were valued at over a quarter of a mill.'

Juliet's jaw dropped. 'You're not serious!'

'Sure am. I borrowed them one day when I was visiting Tregellin and took them into Bodmin. The jeweller there said he'd give me over a hundred thousand for the lot.'

Juliet stared at him. 'But you just said—'

'A valuation is for insurance purposes,' said Cary quickly. 'Selling the rings to a jeweller is something else. Anyway,' he hesitated a moment and then continued doggedly, 'I wondered if you'd be willing to lend them to me, as—as surety for a loan.'

Juliet swallowed. 'I can't.'

'What do you mean, you can't?' Cary had instantly gone from amicable to aggressive.

'I don't have all the rings,' she said. 'I sent the ruby back to Rafe yesterday. It was his mother's ring and—'

'You bloody fool!' Cary was furious. 'Didn't you realise the ruby was the most valuable of the lot? Oh, I know I didn't think so at first, but according to the jeweller it's a very fine Burmese ruby. Apparently, it's flawless and very rare.'

'Well, good.' Juliet was glad they were sitting in the coffee bar when she'd told him. She had the feeling Cary might not be responsible for his actions. 'I'm glad I sent it back to Rafe.' She paused. 'Anyway, if that's all you wanted, I think I'll get back to the shop.'

'But what about the other rings?'

'What about them?'

'Well, are you going to lend them to me, as I asked? You owe me, Juliet. Without that reference I gave you, you probably wouldn't have a job.'

Juliet caught her breath. 'Are you forgetting I fulfilled my part of that bargain? And it didn't cost you a penny, either. Use the money Lady Elinor left you. That must be enough to finance any deal you've devised.'

Cary scowled again. 'You must be kidding! That barely paid my debts.' Then, as she got to her feet, he grabbed her arm again. 'By the way, if you're hoping Marchese will thank you for returning his mother's ring, forget it. Good old Liv is already calculating the odds.'

Juliet didn't believe him, but later that evening, sitting over a ready-made pizza she'd cooked in the microwave, she couldn't help wondering what Rafe would do now. Inheriting Tregellin was a wonderful thing for him, but keeping the old place going was something else.

It was always possible he could do as Cary had suggested when their grandmother was alive and sell one of the farms to gain some capital. There was no doubt that the house needed some immediate renovation, and, although she could understand Lady Elinor's reluctance to face the upheaval, Rafe couldn't put it off indefinitely, not if he wanted the old place to survive.

Still, it was none of her business, she reminded herself. Her involvement had been transitory at best, and she still didn't feel she deserved the legacy Lady Elinor had left her. Her only consolation was that Cary had known about the rings and might have taken them. He'd have sold them without hesitation once his grandmother was dead. Possibly without Rafe knowing anything about it until it was done.

She was washing her dishes in the tiny sink when someone rang the bell downstairs. All the apartments were fitted with intercoms for security, and, although she dried her hands and went to pick up the handset, she was fully prepared for some stranger to have hit the wrong button.

'Hello?'

'Juliet?'

Her mouth dried instantly. 'Yes.'

'May I come up?'

Her hand trembled. She wanted to refuse him. After the way he'd spoken to her at the funeral, she owed him no favours. But the urge to see him again was even stronger. 'All right,' she said, depressing the switch. 'Push the door. It's open.'

In the few seconds it would take him to enter the building and climb the stairs, Juliet made a hasty dash to the bathroom. There was no time to wash her face or no time to change or put on some make-up, but she did run a comb through her hair. She'd worn it in a pony-tail for work and, as usual, she'd tugged off the elastic fastener as soon as she'd got home. Likewise, she'd shed her lacy smock and mini, replacing them with a well-washed pink T-shirt and grey shorts that had seen better days.

He knocked just a few moments later and she hurried back into the living room and closed her bedroom door. Then, barefoot, she padded into the lobby, taking a deep breath before releasing the deadbolt and opening the outer door.

'Hi.'

Rafe stood on the threshold, casually dressed in a black T-shirt and black jeans. Only on him, the clothes assumed a careless elegance, hinting at the taut muscles and lean power they concealed.

But it was the thick sheet of art paper he was holding like a shield in front of him that distracted her. It was a charcoal drawing of herself, half-reclining on a tumbled bed. It was a subtle drawing, innocent, yet sexy. A flattering interpretation of how she must have looked that evening after he'd made love to her.

Juliet swallowed, and Rafe took the opportunity to say, 'It's good to see you, Juliet. Are you going to invite me in?'

Juliet stiffened, trying not to be seduced by his lazy smile. It was obvious that he'd brought the drawing to disconcert her, and he'd succeeded. 'Is there any reason why I should?' she asked tightly. 'I'd have thought I was the last person you'd want to see.'

'Which just shows how wrong you can be,' remarked Rafe drily, his smile fading a little as she continued to block the door. 'Here.' He handed her the drawing. 'This is for you, if you want it. I've got at least a dozen others at home.'

Juliet gasped. 'Do you expect me to believe that?'

'I don't lie,' he said quietly. 'If you'd like to visit my studio again, I'll prove it.'

Juliet chewed on her lower lip for a moment. 'So what do you want?' she asked unhappily, pushing the drawing onto the coat stand just inside the door.

'To talk to you.' Rafe spoke simply. 'To apologise, I guess. I behaved like a jerk at the funeral. You seem to bring out the worst—and the best—in me.'

Juliet sighed. 'Well—OK,' she said, realising she was giving in again. She stepped back to allow him to pass her. 'Go ahead. The living room's through there.'

Rafe stepped inside and she was immediately assailed by the scent of his aftershave, the clean, heated smell of his body. He seemed to hesitate and she stiffened instinctively, but then he walked into the living room, looking about him with an intent dark gaze.

'Do you want a drink?' Politeness was second nature to her and it was a warm evening outside. Besides, it gave her something to do other than notice how much smaller the room seemed with him in it.

'A soft drink would be good,' he said, even though he wasn't driving. But he had the feeling alcohol would just add to his sense of inadequacy.

'Diet cola or orange juice?' she asked, pretending to study the contents of her small fridge. 'I've got both.'

'Orange sounds fine.' Then, noticing she was taking out a glass, Rafe came towards her. 'I'll drink it from the can.'

Juliet hesitated, but it was easier not to argue. Their fingers brushed and she felt tiny sparks of energy shoot up her arm. However, Rafe didn't seem to notice, flicking the tab on the can and drinking thirstily from it. Then he lowered it again and said, 'I needed that. Thanks.'

Juliet made a dismissing gesture. 'Why don't you sit down?' she suggested, the height difference between them pronounced by her bare feet.

He was still an intimidating figure, perched on the edge of the sofa, legs spread, his hands still holding the empty can hanging between. 'Why don't you join me?' He looked up at her enquiringly, but Juliet was reluctant to lose the small advantage she'd gained.

'I prefer to stand,' she said, pulling on the hem of the T-shirt that kept riding up over her bare midriff. 'So—was there something else?'

Rafe's lips twisted. 'Evidently you don't think so.'

'Well, you said you wanted to apologise, and you have. What else is there? Oh—' Juliet frowned as another thought occurred to her. She pushed her fingertips beneath her arms almost defensively. 'I'm glad your grandmother left Tregellin to you. I'm sure you deserve it much more than Cary.'

Rafe looked down at the can he was holding before placing it carefully on the low table near by. Then he leant against the cushions behind him, arms along the back of the sofa, one ankle resting on his knee. 'Was that why you ran away?' he asked mildly. 'Wasn't that a rather childish thing to do?'

'I didn't run away.' Juliet was indignant. 'I never wanted to attend the reading of the will in the first place, and you weren't interested in anything I had to say. I would have liked to say goodbye to Josie, but you and she were talking to the solicitor. I just walked into the village and called a taxi. I already had a ticket for the train back to London.'

Rafe's eyes smouldered a little. 'Did you travel with Cary?'

'No!' She gazed at him warily. 'Did he tell you that I had?'

Rafe shrugged. 'He might have said something,' he responded carelessly. 'I gather you've seen him. Despite your protestations, my cousin appears to play some part in your life still.'

'That's not true.' Juliet sighed. 'If you must know, he came to ask me to lend him the rings your grandmother left me.' And at his narrowing brows, 'I didn't do it. I couldn't. I was afraid that if I'd let him have them, I'd never see them again.'

'Ain't that the truth?' Rafe was sarcastic. 'My God, that man has no shame.'

Juliet considered a moment, and then she said, 'I think he doesn't believe I have any right to the rings. And, in all honesty, neither do I.'

'That's rubbish and you know it.' Rafe got to his feet again, looking down at her with a dark, disturbing intensity. 'The old lady wanted you to have them. All of them.' He put his hand into his back pocket and brought out the velvet box she recognised as being the one she'd sent to him. 'Including this.'

When he flicked the lid on the box, Juliet saw the Burmese ruby nestling on its white satin bed. It sparkled with a life of its own, its circlet of what she now realised must be real diamonds catching and reflecting the light.

'Beautiful, isn't it?' he said, with a peculiar huskiness in his voice. 'Here.' He held the box out. 'Take it.'

'No.' Juliet shook her head and deliberately thrust her hands behind her back. Rafe guessed she was unaware that in doing so, she'd proved to him she wasn't wearing a bra. 'It's yours,' she added, a little of the tension that had been between them in the cemetery sharpening her words. 'It was your mother's ring. No one has more right to it than you do. That's why I sent it back.'

Rafe tried to ignore the hardening in his groin and concentrate on what she'd said. 'So it wasn't just because it was my mother's ring?'

'No.' Nothing could be further from the truth.

He arched an enquiring brow. 'Then, perhaps you sent it back in the hope that I'd return it personally.'

'No.' She was indignant now. 'I wouldn't give you that satisfaction.' She paused. 'Besides, Cary told me that you and— Lady Holderness were—very close.'

'Oh, really?' Rafe was impatient. 'I might have expected something like that from him, but not from you.'

'Why not?' But she coloured in embarrassment just the same. 'You can't deny she knew her way round your apartment. And as for those pictures—'

'The sketches, you mean?' Rafe gave a weary shake of his head. 'I told you about them. She wanted me to paint her portrait for her husband's sixtieth birthday. It was intended to be a surprise. What was I supposed to do? Refuse the commission?'

Juliet caught her lower lip between her teeth. 'So did you do it? Paint her portrait, I mean?'

'Yes.' He shrugged. 'I finished it and she presented it to her husband. Apparently he was delighted, so it's not a secret any more.'

Juliet sighed. 'I'm sorry.'

'Yeah, so am I.'

'You can't deny she—well, she likes you.'

'And I like her. In small doses. Juliet, when I agreed to paint her portrait I hadn't even met you.'

'I know.' Juliet felt ashamed. She glanced towards the lobby. 'The drawing you brought—it's very good.'

'So you're not going to tear it up the minute I walk out the door.'

'No!' She was appalled.

'You sent back the ring.'

'And you know why.'

'Whatever Cary says?'

'Whatever Cary says,' she said fiercely. 'Cary's a liar. I know that now.'

'Oh, yeah.' Rafe closed the velvet box again and placed it on the table beside the empty can. 'But then, he wanted me to fund his overdraft by allowing him to sell the ring. As compensation, as he put it, for depriving him of his inheritance.'

Juliet shook her head. 'But you didn't. Deprive him, I mean.'

'I know. But, like you, I felt some guilt for the way the old lady had treated him.'

Juliet shrugged. 'Most people would consider two hundred thousand pounds more than generous.'

'Yes.' Rafe pulled a wry face. 'But all things are relative, I suppose, and nobody said Cary was cheap.'

Juliet twisted her hands together. 'So?'

'So I offered him the studio and the apartment above it. I said he could either use it as a holiday rental or sell it. I won't need it. I'm having the old coach-house studio where I used to work updated, and I'll be living at Tregellin from now on. Josie says she'll stay until I decide on her replacement. What with all the renovations and such, I couldn't do without her.'

Juliet hesitated. 'So how are you—?' She broke off abruptly. 'Forget I said that. It's nothing to do with me.'

'How am I financing the renovations?' guessed Rafe shrewdly, and Juliet coloured. 'Remember the safety-deposit box old Arnold mentioned?' And at her unwilling nod, 'It contained dozens of investment bonds that the old lady had had since my grandfather died. Arnold said I should cash them in and I did. There was tax to pay, of course, but even so there's more than enough money to restore Tregellin and finance its upkeep for a considerable number of years.'

Juliet's shoulders sagged. 'Well—good. I'm so glad everything's working out for you.'

'Are you?' She was totally unprepared for him to run a slightly unsteady hand over her hot cheek. 'Do you have any real idea of why I came here? Do you know how grateful I was when you returned the ring and I had an excuse to come and see you?'

Juliet quivered. 'Did you need an excuse?'

'After what happened on the day of the funeral? I think so.'

Juliet's nails dug into her palms. 'You were only saying what you thought of me—'

'No!' He shook his head. 'No, I wasn't.'

'Yes.' She licked her lips. 'And I don't blame you. What I did was unforgivable—'

'Juliet—'

'I'm sorry, OK? My only excuse is that at the time I was pretty desperate—'

'As I am now,' Rafe broke in harshly, capturing her startled face between his hands and gazing down at her with frustrated eyes. 'My darling, listen to me. I've regretted every word of what I said a hundred times over. Yes, I was angry with you; yes, I believed you and Cary were still together; and yes, I was blind with jealousy. But it had been a rough couple of months for me and seeing you with Cary just tore me up.'

'I understand.' Juliet gazed up at him. 'Your grandmother's death must have been a terrible shock for you.'

'Yeah, it was.' Rafe sighed. 'I really loved that old lady. But it wasn't just that. Before she died, she told me that my mother's death hadn't been an accident as I'd always thought. She said—she said my mother committed suicide. That when she fell from that balcony, it was a deliberate thing.'

Juliet gasped. 'But how could she know something like that? I thought they were estranged.'

'They were.' Rafe nodded. 'But she wrote to the old lady the day before she died, asking her if she'd look after me.'

'Oh, Rafe!'

'Yeah.' His lips twisted. 'I guess it's not what you expected to hear either.' He paused. 'Does it make a difference?'

Juliet swallowed. 'A difference to what?'

'What do you think?' He shook his head. 'You must know I care about you.' He expelled an unsteady breath. 'Dear God, Juliet, I'm in love with you.'

Juliet could hardly speak. But her hands came up to cover his. 'I don't know what to say.'

'You could say you feel the same,' he ventured softly. His eyes dipped to her mouth. 'Do you know how much I want to kiss you at this moment? Let me kiss you. You don't know it, but you have the most incredible mouth...'

This last was said against her lips, his breath filling her mouth with his taste, his scent. His hands cradled her head, holding her still while his tongue invaded and caressed, showing her how much he needed her with this simple act of love.

And Rafe was a past master at lovemaking. She knew that. But this time he touched her with love, with reverence, and when his finger sought the hem of her T-shirt she was eager to help him. Her insides turned to liquid as he stroked her, his tongue possessing first one swollen nipple and then the other. She was trembling in his arms. She'd longed so much for him to hold her again, and her husky whisper of, 'Of course I love you,' was almost inaudible against his throat.

But he heard her.

'You've no idea how desperate I've been since you left Tregellin,' he said, pulling her closer, letting her feel what her urgent confession had done to him. 'I really thought I'd blown it with you and you didn't even know about my mother. God, I haven't slept since you left me. Not to mention the fact I thought you and Cary were still together.'

'We were *never* together,' Juliet told him fiercely, twining her fingers in his dark hair. 'You do believe me, don't you? And I'm sorry about your mother, but grateful, too. If you'd still been living in Italy, we might never have met.'

'I believe you,' he assured her, his voice thickening as the blood rushed hotly into his groin. A moan vibrated in his chest and he gathered her against him. 'But, dear God, can we save any more explanations until later? I want you, I want to be inside you. Is that a concept you can recognise at all?'

Juliet's lips parted in a delicious smile. 'Oh, yes,' she said. 'I think so.' She paused a moment. 'Would you like to see where I sleep?'

'So long as you understand I don't have sleeping in mind,' said Rafe ruefully. Then he grinned. 'OK, show me. Perhaps I'll think of something else to show you.'

The windows were open in Juliet's bedroom and the muted sounds from the street outside drifted softly on the air. She would have closed the curtains, but Rafe wouldn't let her. 'If anyone wants to watch, let them,' he murmured huskily. 'I love you, Juliet. We've got nothing to hide.'

They undressed each other, slowly at first, but then with an increasing urgency. Juliet's T-shirt and shorts were easy, but it took her slightly longer to unfasten his belt and unzip his trousers.

'Juliet, let me,' he said, his hands shaking a little as he pushed the jeans down his thighs. 'I've had more experience than you,' he added, and she cast him a knowing look. 'Not as much as you think,' he assured her as she knelt on the bed in front of him. 'And I've never said I love a woman before. Except the old lady, of course. But she was something else.'

His mouth on hers was warm and urgent, his hands taking possession of her breasts, his thumbs rubbing sensuously over the hardened peaks. 'You are so beautiful,' he said, regarding her with such reverence that she was humbled. 'I can't believe I let you leave without telling you how I feel about you. My only excuse is, I didn't know you'd gone until afterwards.'

Juliet looped her arms about his neck. 'I couldn't wait to get away,' she confessed. 'I was so sure you must hate and despise me. I wouldn't have blamed you if you had. I hated and despised myself.'

Rafe gave a wry smile. 'And how did you feel about me?'

Her eyes widened. 'Need you ask?'

'I think so.' Rafe nodded. 'After the way I'd behaved.'

'Oh.' She drew back to rest her forehead against his, her smile gentle, her breath warm against his face. 'I think I've been in love with you since that first morning at Tregellin. You and Hitchins came to greet us and I thought you were the most attractive couple I'd ever seen.'

Rafe arched his dark brows. 'Are you sure about that? Hitchins wasn't exactly welcoming.'

Juliet giggled. 'No, he wasn't.' She frowned. 'Where is he, by the way? I'm sort of fond of that little dog.'

'He's at Tregellin. Where he belongs,' said Rafe, and circled her lips with his tongue. 'You'll see him soon enough. He's an amazingly good judge of character.'

But then he couldn't wait any longer. Bearing her back against the pillows, he buried his face between her breasts. 'I love you. So much,' he said, moving over her. 'Don't ever leave me again. I don't think I could bear it. I've filled the house with pictures of you, but they're not good enough. Nothing…' his voice sank to a sensual whisper '…nothing compares to the real thing…'

# EPILOGUE

JULIET'S first Christmas at Tregellin was the happiest she'd ever known. She and Rafe had decorated the old house together, and branches of holly and mistletoe added their own particular aromas to the delicious scent of pine from the huge tree that stood in the hall.

They'd been married in October. The vicar had presided over the service at the small church in Tregellin village with just a dozen or so of their closest friends as witnesses. Then they'd spent a heavenly couple of weeks on an island in the Indian Ocean, before returning to the newly renovated Tregellin House and the life they would share together.

To begin with, Rafe had wanted her to give up her job and go back with him in the summer. But, although it had been a great temptation, she'd decided to complete her computer course. Besides, although he'd told her he loved her, she'd been half-afraid the emotional storm of Lady Elinor's passing had left him feeling vulnerable. She was so worried he'd regret being so impulsive when he'd had time to think.

Of course, she'd been completely wrong. Rafe had spent the subsequent three months travelling back and forth between Tregellin and London whenever his work permitted. He became such a frequent visitor at the apartment that old Mrs Heaton had asked if he'd moved in. 'Given half a chance,' Rafe had assured her humorously, and Juliet had found herself blushing furiously when he'd looked her way.

Since their return from honeymoon, Juliet had virtually taken over the running of the estate. Her newly acquired computer skills had enabled her to format all the accounts, and Rafe had been more than willing to leave the organisation to her.

His own career was going from strength to strength. Several commissions had followed on from his portrait of Lady Holderness, and his talent was being recognised by other galleries around the country. He had so much work that he'd had to cut back on the hours he'd spent teaching, but Juliet was always his first consideration.

As far as they knew, Cary was living in New York these days. He'd left England just after their wedding, leaving a stack of debts behind. Rafe had attended to most of them, despite his solicitor's disapproval. But afterwards, he'd confessed to Juliet that he'd done it for Lady Elinor, not himself.

Then, in January, two things happened that would have an impact on their lives.

The first was that Juliet discovered she was pregnant. She and Rafe had never discussed when they might start a family, and she was a little tentative when she broke the news to him. But Rafe was delighted, if a little anxious about her reaction. 'Do you mind?' he asked her honestly. 'I have to admit, I haven't always been as diligent about using protection as I should.'

'Oh, darling!' Juliet wound her arms around his neck and pressed the whole length of her warm body against him. 'I couldn't be more pleased. I can imagine nothing more satisfying than knowing I have your baby growing inside me. Can you?'

Of course, Rafe took pains to assure her he agreed and by the time they went downstairs again the afternoon was half over. It was snowing outside, the fluffy kind of snow they'd hoped to have for Christmas, and they spent some time watching the flakes falling over the estuary from the windows of the conservatory.

'Just think,' murmured Rafe, drawing his wife's still slim body back against him. 'Next winter, there'll be three of us.' He nuzzled her neck as his hands caressed the slight mound of her stomach. 'So I suppose I should make the most of having you to myself.'

The second thing that happened was totally different.

Towards the end of the month, when Juliet was beginning to suffer the effects of morning sickness, she got a letter from her father's solicitors. It informed her that her ex-husband, David Hammond, had died in George Town in Grand Cayman. He had apparently developed a virulent form of cancer six months ago, and he had made a will making her his only beneficiary.

To say Juliet was stunned would have been an understatement. The letter had arrived as she was making an early-morning cup of tea and she'd had to sit down for a few moments before she could go on. Although Josie still worked part-time at the house, her niece, Connie Boswell, had taken over much of the housework. However, both women were not due to arrive before nine o'clock, so Juliet usually enjoyed this time on her own.

Now, however, she set the cups and teapot on the tray and carried it upstairs to her husband. Despite the efficient heating system, it was still chilly, and she was glad when she could shed her robe and tumble back into bed.

'Mmm, you're freezing,' Rafe groaned as she curled her cold feet around his legs. 'Come here. Let me warm you.'

'Not yet.' Despite submitting to a sleepy kiss, Juliet insisted on wriggling up against the pillows. 'Listen to this,' she added when Rafe started to protest, and, resisting his efforts, she read the letter to him.

'Hell!' The contents of the letter were enough to put Rafe's drowsy appeals on hold. He frowned as he pushed himself up beside her. Studying her pale face, he said, 'Are you very upset?'

'Upset?' Juliet's brows drew together and Rafe thought how utterly delectable she looked, with her nightgown slipping off one shoulder and her hair a tumbled mass of honeyed silk about her head. 'I don't think I'm upset, exactly. Shocked, certainly. He was still so young.'

'Then how do you feel?' Rafe persisted gently, sliding one hand beneath her hair, massaging the back of her neck. 'You look awfully pale.'

'That's 'cos I've been sick again,' confessed Juliet philosophically. And when he started to protest that she should have woken him, she pulled a face.

'What could you do?' she asked, stroking his mouth with her finger. 'Besides, I don't mind, really. Dr Charteris says it won't last long.'

'All the same…' Rafe's mouth compressed for a moment, but when his wife arched her brows he gave in. 'All right,' he said. 'So what about David?' He grimaced. 'The guy must have had a conscience, after all.'

'Mmm.' Juliet was thoughtful. 'I suppose being handed what amounted to a death sentence really focuses the mind.' She sighed. 'I'm sorry, of course. No one deserves to die in those circumstances. But I never loved David.' She gave a tentative smile. 'I know that now.'

Rafe pulled her closer. 'I suppose you'll be a wealthy woman again,' he commented ruefully, but Juliet simply snuggled closer and shook her head.

'I don't want the money,' she said. 'However much or how little there might be.' She reached up to kiss him. 'Would you mind if I donated it to a charity?' And at his smile of approval, 'I've got everything I need right here.'

# REQUEST YOUR FREE BOOKS!

 HARLEQUIN *Presents*

**PASSION GUARANTEED SEDUCTION**

## 2 FREE NOVELS PLUS 2 FREE GIFTS!

**YES!** Please send me 2 FREE Harlequin Presents® novels and my 2 FREE gifts. After receiving them, if I don't wish to receive any more books, I can return the shipping statement marked "cancel." If I don't cancel, I will receive 6 brand-new novels every month and be billed just $3.80 per book in the U.S., or $4.47 per book in Canada, plus 25¢ shipping and handling per book and applicable taxes, if any*. That's a savings of close to 15% off the cover price! I understand that accepting the 2 free books and gifts places me under no obligation to buy anything. I can always return a shipment and cancel at any time. Even if I never buy another book from Harlequin, the two free books and gifts are mine to keep forever.

106 HDN EEXK    306 HDN EEXV

| | | |
|---|---|---|
| Name | (PLEASE PRINT) | |
| Address | | Apt. # |
| City | State/Prov. | Zip/Postal Code |

Signature (if under 18, a parent or guardian must sign)

**Mail to the Harlequin Reader Service®:**
**IN U.S.A.:** P.O. Box 1867, Buffalo, NY 14240-1867
**IN CANADA:** P.O. Box 609, Fort Erie, Ontario L2A 5X3

Not valid to current Harlequin Presents subscribers.

**Want to try two free books from another line?**
**Call 1-800-873-8635 or visit www.morefreebooks.com.**

\* Terms and prices subject to change without notice. NY residents add applicable sales tax. Canadian residents will be charged applicable provincial taxes and GST. This offer is limited to one order per household. All orders subject to approval. Credit or debit balances in a customer's account(s) may be offset by any other outstanding balance owed by or to the customer. Please allow 4 to 6 weeks for delivery.

**Your Privacy:** Harlequin is committed to protecting your privacy. Our Privacy Policy is available online at www.eHarlequin.com or upon request from the Reader Service. From time to time we make our lists of customers available to reputable firms who may have a product or service of interest to you. If you would prefer we not share your name and address, please check here. ☐

HP07

# I ♥

### HARLEQUIN *Presents*

---

## BROUGHT TO YOU BY FANS OF
## HARLEQUIN PRESENTS.

We are its editors and authors
and biggest fans—and we'd
love to hear from YOU!

Subscribe today to our online blog at
## www.iheartpresents.com